J... emb... 1960. Hi... dies... England ... shto... under-Ly... ctrica engineer a... d is hi... second novel.

Praise for Joe Pemberton's first novel, *Forever and E... Amen*:

'An unusually intelligent and beautiful childhood memoir set in Manchester's Moss Side at the end of the sixties . . . *Forever and Ever Amen* describes the adventures of nine-year-old James, in the months before his family move "up in the world" to Ashton-under-Lyne. The youn... hero's vivid imagination blends reality with dreams, nightmare and fantasy, creating a world of bright colour, sensory delight and innocent glee . . . The real delight is Pemberton's easy musical prose. Mundane episodes are twisted through James' eyes into fantastic Hollywood adventures and the dialogue sparkles with natural wit . . . Much of the charm of the novel is in its innocence and lack of cynicism' *The Big Issue in the North*

'A magical depiction of childhood' *Manchester Evening News*

'There are many good reasons to read this book, not least for its insights into a community still little understood in Britain, and for a portrait of Moss Side far removed from its usual "guns 'n' gangs" image. Pemberton's real gift, though, is his evocation of childhood, comical yet never patronising, instantly recognisable to anybody, of whatever culture. Sense of place is strong, and yet the end result is a kind of Mancunian magic realism, strange but familiar, able to hint at large themes even in a small-scale or domestic setting. And best of all, it's also very, very funny' *Third Alternative*

'A first novel with real warmth and an unusual take on childhood' *What's on in Birmingham*

'Pemberton's novel magically recreates a childhood filled with music and fun, sorrow and scrapes' *Belfast Telegraph*

'A lovely book . . . a captivating read' *Woman 2 Woman*

There was this German film on the telly the other night with Liza Minnelli in. Well it wasn't German it was more of a musical actually, for the life of me I can't remember what it was called. It takes place in Germany just before the war, it was that kind of film – the word's on the tip of me tongue. Anyway, there's this geezer at the start and he introduces the shows in the cabaret – did I say most of the action takes place in a cabaret? Didn't I say? Well I'm saying now. Anyway, this geezer, right? He introduces the shows like he's an MC, which he is I suppose, an MC, master of ceremonies, only he's not your communal garden master of ceremonies, not like you get down Cuttles social club on a Friday night. This guy was wearing eyeshadow and lipstick if I'm not mistaken. God, can you imagine them old biddies at Cuttles on the front table having a sight like that all night? They'd have a heart attack, or their money back at least. Mind you, they're always asking for their money back; honestly, there's no pleasing folk, but that's all beside the point really. Think of me as a master of ceremonies, your MC for this book here.

Who am I? A shandy bass in a ladies' glass. That's all I'll say for now. You'll find out soon enough.

Ladies and gentlemen, boys and girls, only it's in German like, and the geezer himself, he's wearing a black suit, dickey bow and a top hat, only he's wearing far too much face powder and lipstick for his own good if you ask me. What time was it on? Oh, after ten I think, I'd set the video to record so I can't remember off-hand exactly. Even so, with that amount of makeup and the way he was dancing, I'm telling you, round here he'd be asking for trouble. Well, how can I put it, it's like me granddad was always saying when he was alive. *In my day*, he'd say, *men were men, women were women, and owt in between got shot*. Saying that, this was the same man whose idea of heaven was a bag of pork scratchings and a warm pint of Theakston's Old Peculiar. It's funny really, now you come to mention, I don't ever remember me gran crying at his funeral last year, or afterwards neither, and since the insurance money's come in, well, we hardly see her now for all these coach holidays she's going on. Where was the last one? Monte Carlo or Cleethorpes or thereabouts, but then I suppose when you're gran's age you're all out of tears.

Mein Herr und Meine Damen, boys and girls; I don't know the German for boys and girls. Actually, I'm only here for the introduction. Afterwards, I'm in the book like the rest of them, so strictly speaking I'm not an MC really because an MC does an introductory speech before each section and I'm beggared if I'm doing that, not on the money they're paying. But that's all beside the point, you couldn't give a tuppence ha'penny one way or the other, could you? I know I wouldn't.

Saying that, if it was up to me there'd be a lot more sex and violence in this book, a bit of blood and bonking never did nobody any harm, think of the sales, that's what I say. Talking of sex, you've heard about whatsisname and whatchamacallit, haven't you? Oh my goodness, in the car park of all places, in front of all and sundry, talk about barefaced cheek, in every sense of the word, too. Don't get me wrong. It's one thing to follow your urges, but it's another matter entirely being spread-eagled across the backseat of a T-reg Talbot Sunbeam in broad daylight, with the car windows open by all accounts, which was asking for trouble considering the traffic at that time of the afternoon. Now, come to think about it, there is your blood and guts, not to mention guns. An AK Kalashnikov apparently. Bet he didn't get that from a catalogue. Darren Molloy Pearson, that's who, the guy in the gun siege, him who gets shot. A headshot by a police marksman, not too dissimilar to President Kennedy's apparently. According to the newspapers anyway. I never knew the guy meself, not that it would have made any difference. A death wish I think they call it. With him holding his wife and kid hostage like that in the middle of the afternoon, in front of all and sundry. Yes, death wish is the only word for it. But that's just typical of some blokes, isn't it? Once they've made their minds up to do something there's no stopping them. And while we're on the subject, what about poor

Clive Barnes? What can I add to what's been said already. Oh, you'll find out soon enough. All I'll say is, have a hanky handy. Still, I suppose you could call it kinky, a man dressing up as a woman every Thursday night. Regular as clockwork apparently. Everyone knows about it but no one says. That's typical of folk round here. So long as you keep your net curtains closed then it's each to their own. Not Clive, silly. Someone else. Who? You'll find out soon enough – patience!

Oh, haven't I said? I must have done. I haven't? Okay, if you say so. From the beginning then. The book takes place in the 1980s, right? And it's an engineering company in the north-west of England, and there's impending redundancies in the pipeline, so to speak. Par for the course really with Thatcherism, the miners' strike, the break-up of trade union power, winter of discontent, Arthur Scargill, *Boys From the Blackstuff*, breakfast television, Roland Rat, that kind of malarkey. Voices, that's it, a bunch of voices. Ordinary folk with ordinary voices, just like you and me. A bunch of northern folk rabbiting on like nobody's business, and no one can get a word in edgeways (a bit like me really), interspersed with a bit of jumping back and forth in time, not to mention jumping from the factory works to a conference centre in a four-star hotel in the middle of the Oxfordshire countryside. And as for the characters, well, there's me best mate Margery. She's an engineer only she goes and gets herself married, doesn't she. Don't get me wrong, James is a nice fella and all and if you're stupid enough to get married in the first place then he's as good as they get, but even so, marriage, for heaven's sake, but hey, don't get me started. Yes, that James, the same James from *Forever and Ever Amen?* The little boy, oh yes, I liked that one, lots of singing and dancing and Technicolor. Only he's not so little now, I can tell you. And like I said, he's as good as they get but in the end he's a bloke like any other bloke, like all the others. Reg Prentice, Matt, and Simon Standage, piss and wind the lot of them – well, I think I've said enough on the subject.

And as for Irene, well, not much going on there. Apart from that Anita Ekberg look that went out in the sixties, well, what can I say? Saying that, have you seen her boyfriend? Toy boy ain't the half of it. More like Dinky toy. Not where it counts, though. Well, it couldn't be; if you see him you'll know what I mean. Personally, I think it's a waste of good material myself. I mean, what can I say without blowing my own trumpet, I'm pretty hot stuff where it matters, not to mention a younger model. I mean, why get a bus when you can fly? Talking of washing, I've a tip for you girls out there in need of a little pelvic stimulation, and no batteries neither. Your local launderette, I'm telling you – the vibrations from sitting on top of one of those toploaders during the spin rinse, oh brother. And you get your washing done at the same time. Got the idea from the telly, one of the soaps if I remember rightly, which is appropriate really. Soaps? Launderettes? Get it? Oh suit yourself. Anyway, have a good book handy, preferably a funny one (you'll know what I mean once you've started), and, oh yes, a spare pair of knickers.

Anyway, I suppose that's about it in a nutshell. A kind of a collective voice piece, a group of your ordinary northern folk really. And all this with a backdrop of back-to-back terraced housing, violence, extreme urban bleakness, civic pride, stereotypical masculinity, poor weather, class, nostalgia, moorland, radicalism, comical regional accents, widescale deprivation; not to mention a sense of space and place, whether symbolic, ideological, emotional, psychological (hey up, how's that for a mouthful).

one

'Joan Collins, yes I'm telling you. Joan Collins, yes her off of that *Dallas* on the telly, here at this very site, well the shop floor actually, but even so, Joan Collins – I wouldn't kick *her* out of bed, ha, chance would be a fine thing. Thirty years ago, well almost anyway, seems like yesterday, don't time fly? Joan Collins, I'm telling you. *Dallas*, or was it *Dynasty* or *Knots Landing*, for the life of me I can't tell the difference, all them shoulder pads, you could breed chickens in them if you'd a mind to. Now there's a thing, that American football lark, what's that about when it's at home? All that grunting and grinding, it's like one of them porno movies, not that I'm into that kind of thing meself. Still, if it keeps the marriage going then who am I to argue? It's good when both of you can share the same interests like, you'll know soon enough. What, you're not courting? Not one of those, are you? That's something at least, still, don't knock it till you've tried it, that's what I say. I prefer racing model boats meself, that kind of thing. The boating lake on Heaton Park just down the road from us, mostly nights and weekends, I've won medals for it.'

It was only one of those massive blue and gold framed pictures of a grey-haired man in all his mayor's regalia sitting in one of those mayor-type ceremonial chairs, the sort of picture seen every day in town halls, foyers and library storerooms, but had James had the chance to swop places with the man stuck up on the wall of Reg Prentice's office there and then he would have done so, no problem. The way the conversation was heading, it could only end in red faces all round. Reg Prentice, Senior Contracts Manager whose jurisdiction included Technical Support Unit, the section where James was due to start that very day, as part of his two-year graduate industrial training. A temporary placement of course, which was kind of a relief, if he was going to have to listen to much more of this kind of thing. Not that he didn't like Reg. James had no doubts whatsoever that Reg was a lovely man, a good father, a wonderful husband, an attentive lover who met his wife's needs both sexually and emotionally, as well as being a dab hand at DIY, barbecues and home brewing. But for goodness sake, he didn't need to hear about it all *now*, thank you very much. Especially on his first day, and on an empty stomach as well. Still, Reg wasn't even half done by the sound of things.

'Folks today, they don't know which side their bread's buttered. In my day you made do with one pair of glasses all your life, even if a lens was missing, what do you think sticky tape's for? Me mother, bless her heart, she had the same pair nigh on forty years she did. Until she passed away. And even then me Aunt Maude, she kept them like, for safe keeping, just in case, next to Granddad's gallstones. Saying that, how do you feel about funeral processions then, fellow-me-lad? I know it's your first day and all, I remember my first day, good grief, yonks ago, I had a hard-on all day I did. I had to wait in the reception room for ages because the manager forgot I was waiting and the receptionist, she was called Brenda if I remember rightly and, well, I'd been to an all boys school, St Lukes on the Preston New Street, they've knocked it down since on account of the foot and mouth epidemic in the sixties, sad business all round. Anyway, this Brenda, Big Brenda they called her, wasn't much of an oil painting herself, oh no. It were that leather handbag of hers. I think they call it a moment of epiphany, yes, that's it. When all the missing pieces fall into place. I could hardly walk straight for the rest of the day, I'm telling you. Had to pretend I'd done me leg in playing football. Anyway, funeral processions, they're a bit of a tradition here. There's one this lunchtime. Clive whatsisface, forget his name, you're his replacement, well temporary anyway. No, don't worry, it's not that kind of job, I can see by the look on your face. Besides, you're too young. Saying that, as an employee you are entitled. A funeral procession past the office gates, we're all entitled, employees of Samson Brothers. Staff, shop floor, cleaners, even management, we're all entitled. So long as the funeral directors are given directions on how to get here. Don't laugh, only last week Stan Tyler's funeral cortège got stranded on the Mancunian Way having taken a wrong turning at Deansgate. It was teatime by the time they'd arrived by the office gates, by which time everyone had left. Sad business all round. It's not compulsory mind you, you might have other plans or your family might object. It's up to each individual. Nobody's twisting your arm, so long as you give a month's notice. Anyway, like I said, it's old Clive whatsisface today, which is good timing if you ask me, seeing as you're his replacement. It'll give you a chance to meet the others in your unit. Kill two birds with one stone as they say. There's one every week, you'll see if you're here long enough, you could set your watches to them. Saying that, I think the record was five in one week, summat like that. With most of the blokes round here it's hardly surprising, seeing as it's their only job since leaving school. Take me for example, not that I would call myself old, would you? No, don't say nowt, it's your first day, wouldn't want to sack you on your first day. I've mine planned already. Reese Macdonald, at the junction of Morton Street as it crosses on to the Welston New Road. You've seen it on your way here? I guess not. Anyway, I'd been walking down the Welston Road the other day after lunch to walk off me dinner. I stops and this hearse pulls over like he's offering me a lift, so I said, "No thanks – I'm not going that far." Only it turns out to be me mate Marty from school who I haven't seen for donkey's years, since school actually, only now he owns that Reese Macdonald and normally he wouldn't be doing the driving only they were short staffed that afternoon on account of the Falklands War on the telly. So we gets talking like, and before you know it he's offering me a twenty-five percent discount on the whole shooting match. Coffin, hearse, flowers, buffet – the lot. Hey, don't laugh, twenty five percent discount less VAT is nowt to sneeze at. And on top of that there's an extra ten percent off if you book the date up to ten years in advance. Margie, Margery, come in, don't wait out there like a lemon, no it's all right, oh suit yourself, stay there then. Margery – whatever you do don't call her Marg, you won't know what's hit you. Lovely girl otherwise, local girl, they all are round here. Not a bad engineer neither, for a girl. Don't tell her that either. She'll have your guts for garters. Personally I haven't a clue about these modern whatnots nowadays. I mean in our day it was all very straightforward. Thermionic valves, transistors, multivibrators, and that's as far as it got. Nowadays, I'm telling you, you blink for five minutes and you're out of date by five years. Anyway, that Margery. Bonny lass and all. Twenty-three years old and not married yet our Marg, sorry Margery. Not even courting neither from what I gather. She'll be past her sell-by date if she don't watch out. A waste of a good figure if you ask me, but still. Not that I'm the slightest bit interested mind you, I've enough on me plate. Oh, look at the time, we'd better be off soon, don't want to miss any of the procession. A bit of a tradition round here. I'll give Margery a shout, you'll see what I mean when you clap eyes on her. Margie, come in girl, I'll introduce the two of you and then we'll be off. I forget . . . Ah Margery, at last, there you are. Margery, meet James, he's here as part of his graduation training – have I got it right? – so mind yourself. Only temporary mind you, not that I blame you, I'd be off like a shot given half the chance. Oh get me, I do go on at times, tell him Margery, hard to get a word in edgeways isn't it, at this rate we'll be here till Christmas . . . Sorry son, I didn't quite catch your surname? Margery, don't stand there like a lemon, you look like you've seen a ghost, for goodness sake woman.'

At the end of the day it's all about acceptance and loving yourself, Margery Watkins was fond of saying to herself. At quiet moments, in the bath or early in the mornings, very early before anyone else has arrived. A few moments to herself with a cheese and Branston pickle sandwich, dunked in a hot, steamy tomato cup-a-soup with croutons. Acceptance and loving yourself; if you can't love yourself then there's no hope, is there?

'And you need to give yourself a bit of love, working at this place,' Margery would say to herself, when no one else was listening.

From now on, a little less pickle, young madam, and some of that low-fat spread from Tesco instead of butter?

'Low-fat margarine instead of butter? Margery Elaine Watkins, how could you?' she would say to herself later on that afternoon when she'd had time to take in the implications of the morning's encounter. Marriage was a big step in a young woman's life, nothing to sneeze at.

But surely she didn't have to give up all the little pleasures in life.

'Margery Elaine Watkins, HND with Distinction, Maltby College, Information Technology Officer for six months now, twenty-three years old, not even close to my sell-by date neither compared to some, and now look at me. Out of the blue you meet the right fella and look at you. Like something out of Mills and Boon. Oh yes, Margery Elaine Watkins. When push comes to shove, you're just like the rest. Oh, and those can't be ticking noises I'm hearing, can they? Surely not. I'm far too young for that palaver.'

Marriage was a big step in a young woman's life and it went without saying that the wedding dress had to be just right. Weddings-Be-Good on the Old Road opposite the swimming baths. If Mother knew what was good for her, she'd better be sat down, with her slippers on at least, later on that night, when Margery gave her the good news.

'Mum,' she'd say, 'it's like you always said, Mum, all along. You *do* know exactly when the right fella comes along.'

And Dad would be just Dad, which went without saying, of course.

'Thank God for that, girl. For a moment back there we thought you were one of those, you know, one of those lesbian fellas you read about in the *Guardian*. We did, didn't we, Mother, go on, tell her.'

'Keep me out of this, you've made your bed now lie in it.'

'Sorry to disappoint you, Father, I can always change me mind.' She always called Dad Father when she wanted to wind him up. Not that he ever took the blindest bit of notice. But he'd be happy enough. She could just hear him.

'I can go down to the Legion now without having the piss taken. I'll pop in later tonight, put that Frank Bates in his place, him and his six grandchildren, two cocker spaniels and his glass eye in a pickle jar on top of the mantelpiece.'

And if things went to plan later that night, and there was no reason why they shouldn't, then Margery and her parents would be spending the rest of the evening planning, remembering to stop at 9.30 because tonight was *Boys From the Blackstuff* and they couldn't tape it because the video was already set for *The Thorn Birds* on ITV. The wedding, the dress, the reception at the Cumberland Suite at the Old Trafford cricket ground that can hold up to five hundred guests for a sit-down meal or a finger buffet. More than enough, even though Dad reckoned that them coloured people always have large families on account of them still going to church and that.

As funeral processions went, this was one of the best for a long while now. The crowd was large too, five rows deep along the pavement, like match day at Old Trafford, all the way from outside the Testing Bay up to the corner shop on Islett Road where they do a lovely corned beef pickle and mustard barm cake for only 20p. The coffin was suitable enough, with just the right amount of brass knobs and polished wood to indicate the person inside was staff and not shop floor, followed by a procession of thirty or so cars, all in various states of upkeep and car registration, ranging from a brand-new blue metallic B-Reg Volvo estate with alloy wheels, right down to a Hillman Imp, three years since its last MOT. And to cap it all off, a squadron of six Hawker Harriers flew overhead in V-formation, followed by a sonic boom as they passed St Margarets secondary modern school. All of which had nothing to do with the funeral procession whatsoever, but then Clive was never one to turn up his nose at any free offers going.

'All this and a sunny day as well, Clive would have been pleased,' said Lorna Smith, one of the canteen staff. She only knew Clive in passing, but any excuse to get out of that hot kitchen.

'Reg, Reg, the copies are done and on your desk waiting. Paper-clipped and double-sided on both sides, headings and footers, I'm telling you, them new-fangled word processors, that fast I'd hardly had time to pull up me tights. And don't talk to me about late post, you can never find a stamp when you want one. Still, there's always mayonnaise, I've a jar in the fridge, I always like to keep one spare in case I run out of salad cream. Ooh, sorry dear, didn't see you there. Oh yes, I can see what Margery means. James, isn't it? My goodness, there was a time when I had all me own teeth, be in there like a shot I would. Don't look so worried, dear. You'll know soon enough.'

Irene Wainwright, fifty-five years old. Secretary to Reg Prentice. From the back you would have thought she was in her mid-forties at the very most. A fulsome figure would have been all the vogue back in the fifties: Marilyn Monroe, Anita Ekberg, Danny LaRue. High heels, a bit too high for an asphalt car park but just right for carpeted corridors, swing doors and gawping eyes from behind the desks and drawing boards.

'Irene, meet James,' said Reg, 'James, Irene. He'll be in the office, only temporary mind you. Bit of a brain box, straight from university aren't you, fellow-me-lad? There's no need to bow, Irene, I said university not royalty.'

'Don't be daft, Reg,' said Irene. 'It's me ankles I'm rubbing, you know me poor circulation. Besides, the word is genuflect; you genuflect to royalty or even the Pope if he's about.'

'Queen, Pope, who cares?' said Reg. 'You look a right prat whatever you call it, and your slip's showing. My goodness, Irene, if I didn't know better I'd say you were doing it on purpose.'

'University of Life, that's me, lad. PhD, BSc, a load of old bollocks the lot of 'em. Don't get me wrong, you seem a nice enough lad, but three years at this place you'll see what I mean. Married with two kids, mortgaged up to the hilt and you'll be having your annual holidays in a caravan at Newquay just like the rest of us, you mark my words,' said Matt Mates, Contracts Draughtsman, based in the same office as James would eventually be. Desk adjacent to the coffee machine and the brand new Samsung photocopier. Just right for starting up a conversation with anyone who happened to be passing. Two written warnings for excessive talking this year already, but no matter; as far as Matt was concerned you might just as well get hung for stealing sheep as lamb.

'The spice of life lad, talking is, social intercourse, the spice of life. Makes the world go round. If God had wanted us to keep quiet he wouldn't have invented dentures. Saying that, I can't abide mayonnaise meself. All that foreign muck. Give me good old British salad cream any day.'

'And you can belt up as well, Matt,' said Irene, 'it's my fridge. Besides, I'm still owed four weeks' milk money. You weren't planning on moving, I hope.'

'I'm only saying, that's all, Irene. It's a free country. I mean, if you like mayonnaise with your chips then who am I to say otherwise? Each to their own, don't you agree, James?'

James just shrugged and smiled. It was only his first day in his first job since leaving university with a BSc in Engineering. So far there seemed to be no reason why he shouldn't stay here for the two years, get a bit of industrial experience under his belt, as they say around these parts. And with even more luck, by then he might just have worked out what the hell everyone was going on about. Not that James was holding his breath. Experience had taught him that the best you could do was a smile and a shrug of the shoulders and if you got home in one piece without too many scars then that was a good day all round.

'Like I said,' said Matt, 'it would be so easy. Joan would run the shop on weekdays. She's been looking forward to leaving teaching for a long time now. The kids today, you need six months in the SAS before they even let you look at a blackboard. But hey, shame about poor Clive, of course you wouldn't know, it being your first day and all. Brain tumour I heard, poor sod, or was it haemorrhoids? Don't laugh, you've never had piles or else you'd know what I mean. His wife phoned in on the Monday with the bad news. Funny thing was, I saw him that Friday by the junction of Welston Old Road and Manchester Road, by the Esso petrol station, you can't miss it, yeah that one, two-pound-fifty a gallon of four star, a rip off if you ask me. I remember thinking to meself at the time that he looked a bit off colour like, more than usual – I know, you could hardly tell with that ginger hair, you wouldn't know of course, not having met him, still, a sad business all around. Clive would have liked that, his replacement being from university and all, even if it is only temporary. What!? Don't look at me like that – the lad's new here, someone has to fill him in with what's gone on, in case he puts his foot in it and says summat out of place. Hey, what have I said now? Hey up, Henry, over here.'

A grey-haired man approached, about fifty-four or thereabouts. Henry Johnson, Chief Technical Support Officer and therefore James's immediate superior. James looked like he needed rescuing from Matt, and besides, it was a good opportunity to introduce himself.

Henry Johnson, Chief Technical Support Officer. Doing

a good job was Henry's only concern, an old-fashioned concept round these parts for as long as he could remember and definitely not a fast-track to the upper rungs of the career ladder neither, but then after twenty years at the same firm you look to get your pleasures elsewhere.

Henry Johnson, Chief Technical Support Officer. Nice enough fellow to have as a temporary boss, it seemed to James, and as bonkers as the rest of them if appearances were anything to go by.

'Take that *Take Your Pick* for example, that quiz programme what used to be on the telly yonks ago, I was saying only the other day, you're too young to remember, yeah, that Michael Miles, *Open the box, that's it*. Anyway, there's this lady with glasses on and she's given the option to open the box, and if you remember, one of the boxes has a booby prize in it and it's an old paint brush – they told you what the prizes were from the start, including the booby prize, only no one knew what was in which box, that was the fun of the game, only this woman she was wearing glasses and all, looked like a school dinner lady, anyway this woman she said right from the start that she was going to win the paint brush. Well, she looked the type, didn't she. Bloody minded for the sake of it. Anyway, this Michael Miles, you could tell he thought she was crackers 'cos he kept on patting her on the head whenever she got a question right. Anyway, when she comes to open the box, lo and behold there was the paint brush, a used one as well, you could tell by the paint stains – I said it was a booby prize – only instead of moaning like the audience did, she whooped for joy, and that Michael Miles he couldn't believe it and he puts his arms around her to reassure her, only she would have none of it. *That's what I came here for in the first place, the paint brush, the booby prize, I'm so happy I could cry,* she whoops, or words to that effect, I can't remember exactly on account of it being black and white telly back then, we didn't even have BBC2, nobody on our street had BBC2 . . . Anyway, I remember she was dead happy, that's all. You could tell she meant it as well, you can't put it on you know, when you're really happy about something, not even on the telly. Anyway, I forget why I'm telling you this in the first place. Oh yes, Ohm's Law, current equals the voltage over the resistance, current times the voltage, voltage over current, whichever way you like, whichever way suits you. Forget all that book nonsense. Ohm's Law is all you'll be needing round here, me lad. Ohm's Law, a screwdriver, a can of loose change, a spare bog roll in your drawer and decent reading material for a long one in the loo. Oh, and when the canteen lady comes to order the morning break bacon toastie, say whether you want tomato ketchup or brown sauce or they'll put nowt on but they'll still charge. Apart from that, anything else is bollocks, you'll find out soon enough. Yes, Ohm's Law, the one you learnt at school, that one.'

And Irene was no better.

'Aye lad, you can fix my taps any time, you only have to ask. As for that Margery, talk about quick off the mark, the little minx,' said Irene as she pinched James on the bottom and winked at him. 'Don't look so frightened, chuck. You'll find out soon enough.'

'Take me Aunt Doris for example,' said Reg. 'She was an active woman, eighty-one years old, always preferred to walk than to catch the bus. I saw me Aunt Doris shopping on the day she died. I was at one stall on the market and she looked a bit off, under the weather like.

'I said, "How are you, Doris?"

'She said, "I can't stop. I'm going to the doctors at three-thirty for a heart monitoring and I've got a lot of pain in my legs – they're killing me. I'll give you a ring tonight to tell you what he said," and off she went. I never saw her alive again. We didn't think much of it at the time, well she was eighty-one and besides, our Doris had no money to speak of. So you can imagine my surprise when I see her GP on the telly. Thank heavens I was sat down at the time. In the end they reckon there were about six bodies at the last count. And to think we thought he was a wonderful doctor; great sense of humour, brilliant at getting into veins. Still, it's a shame about Clive, poor sod. No one had hardly an inkling, I mean, I wouldn't have been on his back so much if I'd known. To think I gave him a right earful about that dockyard job, well, it had been on his desk for ages and I'd had it up to here, it was five minutes before clocking off and there was still no sign of the report on me desk, it's no surprise harsh words were said. But you can't take it back, can you, ho hum.'

'And that's not the half of it neither,' said Matt. 'If you ask me things have been going to pot for a long time now.'

According to Matt, it used to be quite a fun day out, a family picnic on t'moors. Pack the kids in the back of the car along with a hamper, a cricket bat and football, a transistor radio and a couple of Mills and Boon and a pack of cards just in case. That would be it for the day, a fun day out of fresh fields, lots of sheep and the occasional rambler asking directions for the nearest pub. As the night crept in it was out with the spade and bucket and after five minutes' digging there would be enough peat for a winter's worth of fuel.

'But they put a stop to all that, they did, that couple who buried all them kiddies on t'moors. Folk round 'ere don't like to talk about it much,' said Matt, as he wiped away an imaginary tear.

'You know, for a time to come those two have spoilt a lot of good things for a lot of folk – a glass of wine, music on the wireless, holiday snaps, ball games – oh they've done their work all right – a right pair of miscreants, them two.'

All of which was fine by James. Reg Prentice, Irene, Henry, Matt, standing out in the pouring rain watching the funeral procession of the guy he was meant to replace, only temporarily. And that Margery girl who kept on looking at him like she'd found something. It wasn't everyday that a good-looking woman stared at him like that, if ever. It was him that usually did the staring, after which they would do a runner. And if truth be known he wasn't so sure how to take it, this Margery doing the staring. Still, she was bloody good looking, that was for sure. Hopefully, she wouldn't stare so much the next time they met. Give him the chance to say hello or something. Still, by the size of the funeral, you couldn't blame James for getting the impression that Clive must have been someone quite important. Matt and Irene put him straight right away.

'What, Clive? Are you kidding?' said the both of them in unison before collapsing with laughter, and it was at least another five minutes before either of them had sufficient breath to carry on a decent conversation with anyone never mind James.

'It's the lad's first day, he isn't to know,' said Henry. 'Behave yourselves you two, honestly.' Then he turned to James. 'Take no notice, you'll get used to them in time. Besides, being laughed at is what you call a term of endearment round here. It means they like you.'

And when neither Irene nor Matt responded, Henry then went on to explain to James that this size of funeral procession was nothing out of the ordinary, pretty much bog standard really. Neither was it unusual for there to be at least three processions a week. With there being over one thousand five hundred employees at the last count, and other factors such as overhead power lines, women smoking when they're driving, drinks served in short measures, fluoride in the water, that bloody Maggie Thatcher and the rest of that lot, well, it stands to reason, doesn't it, lad.

'Take Albert Porter for example,' said Matt. 'Forty-five years in Packaging and Casings. Heart attack last month, collapsed right in the middle of lunch break. Steak and kidney pudding all over the place; if you look carefully, you can still make out the stains on the walls. Anyway, his procession, you think this is big, ain't even half the size. The management were that close to calling the police in case of crowd trouble, it were that bad. Wasn't it, Irene? Albert Porter's procession last week, bloody enormous it were.'

'I bet it is,' said Irene, as she pinched James's bottom again. 'Now you've gone and done it, young man, I'm all moist now.'

two

Henry's Makeup Tips 1 Beard Cover by Henry Johnson

Introduction

It's like most things really. Ninety percent of the work goes in to the preparation. And if you ask me, it's not that different to decorating the house in many ways. Plastering, painting, wallpapering, that kind of thing; you need a smooth surface to begin with. And you know what it's like if you cut corners: paper continually falls off, the paint peels after a couple of months and you have to do the whole lot again. Meanwhile all the shops have run out of that particular patterned paper you'd found a roll of in the loft when you first moved in, and the only place that sells it now is an arts and crafts shop in Heaton Chapel at £10.50 a roll.

(1) Let your beard grow

Okay, it's a Thursday morning and a brand-new outfit has just arrived through the post – bear with me here, I'm trying to create a mood. Well I can tell you now it's away with the shaver for the day. And I keep it that way *all day*, until the evening, just before tea about six-thirty. I know, if you're like me you're like a bear with a sore head when you haven't had a shave for the day, but believe me the results speak for themselves, trust me.

(2) Pluck what you can

Before I shave I pluck out the hairs over my upper lip with tweezers. And none of those plastic tweezers neither, waste of good money. Metal ones, one of those stainless steel jobs, tips sharp enough to slice corned beef. Yes, and before you start whingeing, you think that's bad, try having your legs waxed. I'm telling you, I'd have broke the record for high jump if someone had had a tape measure handy. Trust me, plucking your moustache with tweezers pales by comparison. Don't get me wrong, it brought tears to my eyes at the start, but it's like the wife always says, if it was left up to men to have babies . . .

(3) Shaving

I know what you're thinking. Been doing it since your voice broke. Still, you'd be surprised how many of us don't actually shave properly or with the right kind of razor. And I'm telling you, the last thing you need is a face full of cotton wool when you're all dressed up in your favourite Laura Ashley. The important thing here is to have a good flexible razor and a light cover of shaving cream. Not thick, but slippery. I use skin cleanser myself – Boots' own brand, inexpensive and you can buy it over the counter without the shop assistants raising their eyebrows. Just enough to make the skin as slippery as the surface of a bar of soap. Shampoo does the trick too. Once, I was that desperate I even used Swarfega. The soap the engineers use on the shop floor, you must have heard of it. Lethal stuff – it has to be to cut through all that oil and grease. I always keep a spare bottle handy in the bathroom, for washing me hands after doing the car or the garden. Anyway, wouldn't have touched it with a bargepole for me face ordinarily, but I'd overslept and was in a rush and out of shaving cream, and me wife had forgot to put out a new bar of soap and the Swarfega was there, and you know what they say, needs must, so just the one squirt and a quick rub and it worked a treat, like a baby's bottom me face was afterwards, I'm telling you. Not sure I'd risk it again mind you, I'd end up looking like Ed Bains from Accounts. Psoriasis since he was a kid, he's even been in hospital with it. Think *Singing Detective*, yes that telly programme. Anyway, where was I? Shave with slow downward strokes all the way around – like this, see? Then go back and shave against the grain, I repeat, against the grain – whichever way that is. Continue rubbing your face and looking for any rough spots and go over them again.

(4) Stop the bleeding

Easy to do at the best of times as you well know. The traditional methods are the best, cold water, aftershave, whatever suits you, though I prefer cold water myself. Imagine Old Spice with your favourite I've San Laurent? Doesn't bear thinking about.

(5) Apply lipstick

There, that stopped you in your tracks. Apply lipstick where you can see shadow. Use your fingers to rub it in. It's amazing what you can do with lipstick – we'll come back to it in our 'Lips' section.

(6) Apply concealer

Apply a yellow concealer – that skin-coloured stuff that comes in sticks, you know, that women use to cover blemishes and birthmarks – over the red lipstick and blend. Boots' own brand again is all you need. And don't forget, if you feel uncomfortable in shops asking for this or similar items, try home-order catalogues, I swear by them myself. You'll be surprised by the range. Use your wife's name, or your girlfriend's – as long as they already know, of course. I prefer general catalogues to the more specialist ones, seeing as my tastes are more conventional, shall I say. At my age you can't afford to take risks, trust me. You might want a Mona Lisa look but will probably end up looking more like a bad Picasso, on a rainy day, and you left your brolly at home.

(7) Apply liquid makeup

The key here is to choose the same shade of liquid makeup and powder. Both should match your skin tone. If you have trouble matching your skin tone, ask someone to help you out – that's if you can, mind you; the last thing you'd want is to let the cat out of the bag, so to speak, all for the sake of a bit of liquid makeup. Apply the liquid makeup – or foundation, as it's sometimes known – with a triangular sponge, using up strokes rather than down. Blend in with the concealer. Use the edges of the sponge to help smooth away any clumps or streaks. Also remember to refresh your makeup. Just because you haven't run out doesn't mean you don't need to replace it. Personally, I invest between £5 and £10 every eight months or so. It's money well spent in the end. If you're going to pay top whack for any cosmetic item it should be your liquid makeup, followed by mascara and powder.

A good tip I once learnt from a magazine: put the liquid foundation on your eyelids as well, because this will help your eyeshadow last longer. We'll come to eye makeup later, but again Boots do a nice range. And of course, there's always the catalogues, as I said; some of them even do next day delivery, so what more can you ask?

(8) Apply powder

Blot the powder, don't rub it in, you'll see what I mean with a bit more practice. And use the applicator, not a dusting brush, that comes later. The purpose of this stage is to soften the appearance of the face and set the foundation. But don't put it on your eyelids, you're saving them for the eyeshadow later. Watch this space, as I said.

(9) Look at yourself

Take a long, hard look at yourself in the mirror – hey, it's too late to be coy now – preferably in a bright light, and apply concealer and powder where necessary on those trouble spots.

And don't be discouraged. The tricky bit's behind you and you're well on your way to creating the perfect face. It's like that Mr Kipling said, *If you can keep your head while all those about you are losing theirs, then you'll be a man, my son.*

three

Matt shook his head in disbelief.

'Let me see if I've heard this right, Clive, I may have missed something. There's a man in your bedroom, a man who you've never met before, and it's one o'clock in the morning – you know because the weather report on Radio Four has just ended and the radio's playing the national anthem as always after the weather report. And this man, he's standing over your bed and he asks to use the toilet. And his name was Charles, right?'

Clive shook his head.

'No, Carl not Charles. I made that mistake as well. He got right peeved.'

The phone rang. An intermittent tone, therefore an internal call.

'Hello, yes. Matt Mates speaking.'

'Matt, my man, how's things?' said Mike Trent.

Mike Trent from Designs. Quarter past ten, mid-morning tea break. So it was either a Twix, KitKat or a

Toffee Crisp, if there were any left. Hence the phone call.

'Matt, my man,' said Mike. 'Say you haven't run out of Toffee Crisps.'

'Dunno, Mike, you know what it's like this time of the week. You'll be lucky if there's any Smarties left.'

'Come on, Matt, stop pissing about.'

'Peanuts, Liquorice Allsorts, and what's this, a Sherbet Dip?'

'For fuck's sake, Matt. I'll send Irene to collect *two* Toffee Crisps in ten minutes, right? We'll settle up later in the Chickens Nest. Hey, and if you get there first, get a seat near the telly, golf's on. See you then.'

Matt put the phone down.

'Thanks, Matt, it was my pleasure, Matt. You know me, Michael, here to serve. So, Clive, where were we up to? There's this bloke, Charles or Carl, and he's standing by your bed and he asks to use your toilet and it's the middle of the night, one o'clock in fact, you know because you looked at the clock, and you've never met him before in your life, right? Had Maureen? Hey, keep your shirt on, Clive, I was only asking . . . Hang on, the damn phone, don't they know it's tea break . . . Hey George, my man. How's tricks, George? I was thinking about you only the other day and I know you don't like mentioning it at all but I was saying to the wife it's been almost twenty years now or thereabouts, hasn't it, correct me if I'm wrong?'

Not that George could give a monkey's one way or the other. Like Matt said, it was almost twenty years ago now, twenty years three months two days, or thereabouts, since his best mate at apprentice school became the last victim of that couple who killed all them kiddies on t'moors. And from that time on, mothers and fathers would warn their children not to talk to strangers, even those offering sweets and ice-cream cornets. In fact, life was never quite the same again. But if Matt wanted to bring the subject up then it was fine by George. Besides, he was only after a packet of Polos, if not then Trebor Extra Strong, or even Tic-Tacs; anything minty, he wasn't fussed.

'Hang on, George, I'll ring you back later. Summats brewing here.'

By the time Matt put the receiver down, Alan Wise had already cleared out his desk and was about to pack his briefcase – all of this under the watchful eye of Simon Standage, Assistant Personnel Director for six months now, with an office in the executive suite, accompanied by two security guards, recently hired from PrimeForce, the local security firm at the back of Lime Street as it crosses the Welston Old Road.

'For fuck's sake,' said Matt to himself, looking over to where Alan Wise, the Senior Sales Engineer for Overseas Sales usually sat. Even the security guards were quite embarrassed, but then they were under strict instructions, and besides, at £1.50 an hour they weren't being paid enough to think, never mind care. And anyway, if the rumours were true about the whole place being demolished and replaced by a greyhound race track, then all this would be a walk in the park compared to what was in store.

Alan Wise was almost in tears by now. Twenty-five years' experience counted for nothing nowadays.

'I can't pack so quickly,' said Alan, 'I'll have to come back tomorrow.'

But Simon Standage was having none of it.

'You should have thought of that before getting that job at Saltshafts. When I say *leave the premises right now*, I mean *right now*. Do I make myself clear?'

It had been almost two weeks now since Alan had been offered the job at Saltshafts. Senior Test Engineer and on three grand more. Not that Alan had wanted to leave. All he'd wanted was to test things out, maybe squeeze an extra rise out of the Management. It wasn't like he was the first or anything like that, setting a precedent as Reg Prentice would say. But since those two Americans were brought in from the States, well, nothing was the same any more and everything was up for grabs now.

'Five minutes,' said Simon Standage, 'and if you're not out by then I'll set these two monkeys on you, see if I won't.'

Poor Alan Wise, definitely in tears now, which was a shame really, especially for someone with his experience. Not that any of that mattered nowadays.

'You heard what I said, *five minutes!*'

As stories went, the one about Alan Wise being given five minutes to clear his desk and to leave the premises immediately was par for the course lately. Not that it made the slightest difference to Joan, Matt's wife, who'd been in bed since nine o'clock as there was never anything much on the telly on a Tuesday. All she wanted was a good night's sleep, for a change. But that was out of the question with her husband all worked up like this.

'I mean,' said Matt, 'Alan Wise, twenty-five years service altogether at Samson Brothers, if me memory serves me right. I mean, Alan Wise of all people, the man was married to the place and now this, I mean, what can I say? Alan Wise, crying for heaven's sake. Twenty-five years' experience down the pan like that, I'm telling you, a right can of worms if you ask me, the Management haven't a clue what they've let themselves in for. That Simon whatsisname, he'd better watch his back if he knows what's good for him. I'd have fisted him meself if I weren't on the phone, I'm telling you I'm serious, I mean it, don't laugh, it's not funny.'

None of which was any surprise as far as Joan was concerned, what with the stories she'd been hearing of late.

'So, Matt, have I got this right? There's this man in Clive's bedroom who he doesn't know from Adam and it's one o'clock in the morning because the radio's playing the national anthem and this man, he wants to use the toilet, only he doesn't know where it is so he wakes up Clive to ask. And where's Maureen whilst all this is happening? Oh, she slept through the whole thing, well that figures.'

four

Darren Molloy Pearson. Twenty six-years old, he hadn't a clue who Alan Wise was, didn't care about Mars Bars, Polo mints, or Matt's wife Joan for that matter. Unless they had anything to do with heating the milk for the Ready Brek, hoovering the living room carpet, dressing Darren Junior and walking him to school with the other dads, then they would all have to wait in the queue like everything else. While he was busy with Darren Junior, Karen, his wife, got herself ready for work. Chambers Upholstery in Glossop, an upholstery machinist, leather suites and sofas, £2.50 an hour, with the overtime and time-and-a-half on Saturdays, the money had to come in somehow. And at £2.50 an hour, with time-and-a-half overtime on Saturdays, even Darren had to admit it made more sense for him to do the cooking and cleaning. Not that he would ever complain. He was good like that was Darren. Karen couldn't tell him off about that at least. Not that she made a habit of telling him off of course, she was also good like that. Besides, they always made it to school on time. Kingshill Primary, just across the road from Darren's parents' house on Addison Street, just by the junction with Welston Old Road. Darren's old school when he was Darren Junior's age. In those days you wouldn't be seen dead going to school with your parents, never mind your dad.

Pleasures were a lot simpler when Darren was Darren Junior's age. A free bottle of milk, 2p for a chocolate Dundee biscuit, like a chocolate digestive only bigger and thicker, as well as dinnertimes, especially if it was chips. Or when it was almost the summer holidays when lessons would be cancelled and days were spent on trips to Chatsworth House, Lyme Park or Jodrell Bank, depending on where they had been last year, as well as sports days in the field at the back of the school where the headmistress would come out from the office without her cloak and gown, and after handing out the cups to the winners would return to her office at the back of the school and no one would see her again until next year.

When Darren was Darren Junior's age you wouldn't be seen dead going to school with your mum or dad. Not that they would have had the time to take him even if they'd wanted to, with having to work and all. Not that things had to be this way for Darren, according to his dad.

'You only have to say, and I'll have a word with Personnel.'

But Darren had his own ideas. Darren has *always* had his own ideas, as his father was always saying. Not that it would have made any difference in the end anyway.

Especially with all the rumours going around about redundancies.

Darren Molloy Pearson, Molloy after one of Dad's favourite films. One of those black and white films from the sixties with Sean Connery. Sean Connery was Dad's favourite. Ever since *Goldfinger*, when one of the Bond girls got sprayed with gold paint all over.

'A man's man,' Dad was always saying, which was funny really because if it had been left up to Dad, then Molloy would have been Darren's first name instead of Darren. Darren had Mum to thank for that. She said the boy would be teased at school by all his mates and that was the end of it.

With a little care and attention, a pack of self-rolled cigarettes can be made to last a long time. And so long as the chores were done then everyone was happy. Monday mornings was bins out by 10.30, preferably the night before, unless the neighbours' car was in the drive all day. And how many times must he tell Karen: the living room bin was only meant for papers and such, not orange peel, apple cores or cotton buds. The smell in the mornings the next day – talk about stink. It was okay for her, having to rush to work in the mornings and not have enough time to listen to a word he was saying. Washing day twice a week, whites Tuesdays – look after the whites and the pounds look after themselves. And even Karen had to admit his cooking was much better by a mile. Especially since he bought the wok from the Chinese stall at the Ideal Homes exhibition at Belle Vue, a pretty good buy even if he said so himself, not to mention the gallon bottle of soy sauce and other assorted condiments that went with it – twenty percent off with the ticket stub. So in the end, the day could go by pretty quickly, with a little careful planning, or would drag so much he might just as well stay in bed and put up with the earache from Karen when she got home from work.

'Which is a pity because heaven knows we could do with the extra money coming in, with Christmas and everything, you know how it is. Still, Darren tries his best, you can't say fairer than that. But it gets to you in the end.'

However, Darren was always open to suggestions on making the day go quicker. And his mother was always on hand to give such advice, whether by phone, or if she just happened to be passing, or on their regular Sunday afternoon visit, which meant that for at least one day of the week the family had a fresh cut of meat. Roast beef usually or sometimes lamb or occasionally a large chicken, always with gravy and Yorkshire puddings.

'I couldn't do without those little luxuries,' Darren's mother would always say. 'I'd go mad otherwise. You try staying home all day.'

So every weekday at a quarter past one, it was a large pot of hot steaming tea with all the milk and sugar in the mugs beforehand. Six teaspoons with the big pot, four-and-a-half with the ceramic one kept under the sink. A large plate of cheese crackers with maybe a slice of cucumber or tomato or even celery, depending on what was left in the fridge. And in no time at all it would be three o'clock and it was only a five-minute walk to the primary school just across the road from his parents' house on Addison Street, just by the junction with Welston Old Road. When Darren was Darren Junior's age you wouldn't be seen dead going to school with your mum or dad. Still, there was always the Dundee biscuits to look forward to: 2p was pretty cheap even for those days.

And even back then when he was Darren Junior's age, Darren knew what he wanted when he grew up. A brand-new house, a pretty wife who could cook, and a car, and not just any car neither. A brand new white Mini coupé like the ones advertised on the telly and the large posters outside the school – that was all. And everyday he'd have a breakfast of toast and marmalade and black coffee because being a grown-up meant you could drink black coffee without asking permission, with his pretty wife of course, who had long blonde hair and dimples, looking a lot like Susan Moore in his class, only a grown-up. After which he would leave for work in his T-shirt and brown corduroy trousers. And his pretty wife would wave to him from the bathroom window, and he'd wave back, long enough so the neighbours could see him, but not too much in case he got cramp. And then he would get into his brand-new white Mini coupé, bought on hire-purchase because being a grown-up meant you do this too, without asking permission. And it went without saying that it would be a sunny summer's day, which was just as well seeing as his job was working outdoors as a draughtsman at the fairground at Belle Vue designing funfair rides for amusement parks throughout the country and beyond, even Disneyland and Hollywood. And he'd have his own drawing board and pencils and pens with his name on so that nobody could steal them. Yes, Darren knew exactly what he wanted to be when he grew up, even back then when he was Darren Junior's age.

Still, where there was hope, and now when the weather was fine and if there were enough dads about, which was always the case nowadays, there'd be a kickaround outside by the bike shed wall, just like they'd had when they were Darren Junior's age. And before long there'd be enough for two teams, with the rolled-up coats and two piles of old milk crates and workman's cones from the building site for goals – a bit Heath Robinson but it did the trick. A lot like old times really.

five

Even so, there should have been a message, a warning perhaps, on a plaque, in bold print so no one could miss it even if they wanted to. Something like:

Use the lifts at your own peril !!

Not that Henry would have taken the blindest bit of notice the mood he was in. Thursdays were never the best of days for Henry. Everyone had come to expect as much, but thankfully by Friday things would be back to normal and Henry would once again be his calm, familiar self, like butter wouldn't melt. And no matter what the problem, he would be only too pleased to help because he was like that was Henry, courteous and friendly, like, except on Thursdays. And most of them knew why as well only no one was saying. There wasn't any point really. Let sleeping dogs lie and all of that. Still, this was Thursday and Thursdays were never the best of days for Henry.

'Fucking bastards,' said Henry, 'fuck fuck fuck.'

'The language in here,' said Irene, 'you could sell tickets.'

'Cut it out, will you?' said Matt. 'There's ladies present.'

'Who you calling a lady?' said Irene. 'Cheek!'

'Sorry, our Irene,' said Matt. 'No offence meant.'

'Just you watch yourself next time.'

Henry's red face looked set to explode any minute now, temples throbbing and nostrils steaming to match.

Matt tried again. 'I'll go down myself, it's on the way to the buttie bar anyway. Kill two birds with one stone. Corned beef, is it?'

'No,' screamed Henry, 'corned beef, ham, cheese, meat paste and sandwich spread and in that order as well or you can take it right back. And while you're at it, go fetch that work instructions file from Purchasing. And get a move on, sharpish, like.'

'What did your last slave die of? OK, I'm off.'

Meanwhile, back in the ground floor lobby, the lift had stopped about halfway between the first and second floors, thus making escape impossible. And judging by the screams, shouts and bangings there was someone trapped inside.

'Let me out, I can't breathe!' screamed whoever it was.

A crowd had gathered by the lift doors, which was against company regulations – a memo posted up stated that under no circumstances must employees gather outside the lift in the event of it breaking down, or words to that effect. Only now it was hard to make out exactly what it *did* say, with all the scribbling, chewing gum and a *Support the Miners* sticker.

'Someone ring for the engineer?' asked Shaun Hughes, Design Draughtsman for seven years last March, who was due for an interview for the vacant Section Head spot that coming Friday so it was best to show willing just in case any Management happened to be passing. If he'd remembered that most of the senior managers were away on that two-day conference at Holme Lodge then he would have saved his breath and just stood and had a good gawp like everyone else. Any excuse for a good chin-wag.

As usual, everyone was doing the listening and one person all the talking. In this case it was Martha Westinghouse, forty-nine years old, Tracer for ten years, with one agenda up until three months ago – the menopause, hot flushes, wet bedsheets, unsympathetic husbands and everything else that went with it. In some ways it was quite a relief for everyone to have Martha doing the talking. All they had to do was listen and nod in the right places. Though she didn't half go on.

'I only popped out for a bag of sugar and the next minute I come back and there's fire engines, police cars and all sorts. Daft buggers, they'd only gone and gotten the addresses mixed up. That young couple across the road, number twenty-two, ours is twenty-one you see, only you can't tell because of the herbaceous borders, easy enough mistake to make. Postmen are always getting it wrong, you'd think after all these years they'd know by now, still, if they insist on changing postman every five minutes. The council are footing the bill so that's something at least, mind you, there would have been Mary hell to pay if they hadn't, the state of our lawn afterwards, worse than the battle of t'Somme, and don't mention the Somme with Granddad about, he never shuts up. I know he's old and everything and if it were up to me he'd have the box room upstairs, turn it into a granny flat, you know, but it's the children. Our Tracy just turning fifteen and with Kevin and his football practice, well, it would never work. Besides, Sunday lunch once a week that's more than enough, some of them old folk at the home don't see their family for donkey's years so there you go, still, I wish he wouldn't go on about it so – t'Somme this is – it upsets everyone so, two glasses of Sanatogen wine and there's no stopping him, trouble was he was only in the catering corp, not that you'd have any idea, talk about walking wounded, he'd have you believe he was the only one wounded. I wouldn't mind but it's only a bit of metal in his backside, but oh does he go on, a martyr to moving shrapnel, that's what our Tracy calls him. Not to his face, mind you, we'd never hear the end of it.'

The gathering was so big now that they could have held a union meeting right there and then if anyone had had a mind to, and none of the Management would have been any the wiser. Had the Management been on the premises, of course, and not at the Holme Lodge Hotel in the middle of the Oxfordshire countryside. Not Mutt and Jeff, of course. They had more important issues in hand, which involved hiding round corners and appearing out of nowhere all of a sudden. Anywhere, any place, any time, the more inappropriate the better. And if the poor unfortunate was to almost have a heart attack then all the better. Take Janine Taylor from Tracing for example. She'd only just flushed the toilets and was in the process of pulling up her tights when Mutt and Jeff popped out from the next-door cubicle to ask if she'd heard the rumours about the company being closed down in two weeks' time in preparation to develop the site into an abattoir for the whole of Greater Manchester by September 1987.

And later on that same evening, long after the police, fire engines, ambulances and the TV crew had left, Matt and his wife would watch edited highlights of the day's proceedings on the local evening news on both channels – the one on ITV being extended for an extra fifteen minutes so *Wish You Were Here* had to be cancelled for another date, which nobody minded too much really as it was only Judith Chalmers again on yet another Caribbean cruise.

The *Manchester Evening News* wasn't much better – the report of a striking miner being killed by a lorry was put back to page five. And if the front page and the headlines weren't enough there was a six-page special pull-out section devoted entirely to the siege on Acomb Street.

'I'll keep it for a souvenir,' said Matt's wife, Joan, later on that same evening in bed watching the telly, with Matt already asleep. 'Might be worth a bob or two in a couple of years time.'

Still, a gunfight and siege on Acomb Street didn't happen every day. The first time anyone had an inkling that something was amiss was when a bullet smashed through the Designs Section on the second floor, just missing Dennis Mottram's head by inches, before smashing into the wall behind him right above the picture of his favourite page three girl, Debbie-Marie Monroe.

'I almost wet meself,' Dennis said later on that evening at the Samuel's Arms after his fourth gin and tonic. 'I mean, it's not what you expect on a Thursday just before elevenses. Yes, I'll have another double gin and tonic, only this time forget the tonic, and the ice.'

Things happened so quickly after the first bullet smashed through the window. More bullets, followed by flying glass and bits of salmon sandwiches. Doris Burke fell to the ground so quickly she couldn't miss the buffet tray of sandwiches, cakes and vol-au-vents specially prepared for the meeting in Andy Barrett's office.

'Hey up,' said Doris at the time, 'that's me second pair of tights ruined this week.'

The initial bullet was followed by the rat-a-tat-tat of more bullets and a great big thud. And almost immediately the sirens and car alarms went off as if to say, *Hey, we can make as much of a racket as well, you know*.

Doris Burke was almost beside herself with excitement as she ducked under her desk to escape the flying bullets and plaster. 'Could murder a bag of chips right now. I'm like this when I'm all excited. When there's an action film on the telly, a pound to a penny there's nowt left in the fridge by the end of the film and next day it's a trip to Tesco.'

And at the end of the day, when all the dust had settled bar the shouting, it was a miracle that the only serious injury sustained was to Len Fairley, one of the accountants on the ground floor, who had to stay overnight at Woodside General Accident and Emergency after being given a bloody good hiding when he was caught in flagrante as they say with Nora Wainwright, one of the machinists from Windings. Nora Wainwright, the wife of Norman Wainwright, from the Millers Department, small bloke but calf muscles like whip-cords, who once the evacuation had started had grabbed at the chance to pop home sharpish like, to check up to see how his sick wife was faring, having decided to stay in bed that morning on account of having yet another one of her heads.

But none of this had transpired yet, and back in the offices Matt looked at Henry and Henry looked at Matt and everyone looked at everyone else, wondering what the hell was going on up there to make such a racket, and just as immediately the fire alarms went off followed by the rumblings on the stairs because it was pretty obvious to everyone that this was no fire drill and no mistake. And just in case there was anyone left with any doubts about what to do, the message over the tannoy put a tin hat on it all.

'Please vacate the building. This is not a fire drill, I repeat, this is not a fire drill.'

Just for good measure, there was another announcement over the tannoy warning that if there was anyone caught idly chatting away then they would be sacked on the spot immediately – words to that effect, near as dammit. Simon Standage, the new Assistant Personnel Director, who had seen his opportunity to make his mark while all the other senior managers were away at Holme Lodge. And that had been his only intention, just a chance to enhance his career prospects even further, that was all, nothing more sinister than that, but it was a well-known fact that the road to hell was paved with good intentions.

It could have been a scene from Dunkirk or the Normandy beach landings or Hitchens during the New Year sales, or even many years later when the IRA blew up Marks and Spencer and most of the city centre. Almost the whole of the workforce had gathered in the car park by now, just walking in an orderly fashion or waiting patiently for further instructions. There was even the St John's Ambulance with a big flask of tea in case anyone took a turn for the worse. Some say it was a bit of an overkill really – no pun intended – seeing as the shooting was taking place in one house in one street and there was only one gunman and one gun, and so what if it was a Kalashnikov, no harm was intended. Even so, the police decided it was best not to take any chances, especially as the gunman was once a reservist in the Paras. However, none of this was of any concern to Simon Standage, back in the car park where the whole of the workforce had now assembled. This was his moment to make a great impression, to make his mark as they say. A window of opportunity. A chance like this only comes up once in a lifetime, if that. Seize the day, or as they say round these parts, *You're a long time dead, chuck.*

Simon Standage, married six years, with a little girl called Sadie, two years old, and a detached house in Marple Bridge, even more determined to consolidate his new position as Assistant Personnel Director, appointed six months ago. So with a megaphone in one hand and his other hand waving about like nobody's business, he directed the gathering crowd of employees into their respective sections so that a name check and a head count could eventually be made.

'Single file I say, single file,' screamed Simon through the megaphone. 'The quicker we get this over and done with the quicker we can all go back inside.'

If only Simon had left matters as they were and not rubbed people's backs up so much that they had no choice but to go out on a lightning strike like that. If only there hadn't been so many police marksmen in the street. If only Darren Molloy Pearson hadn't found that five-pound note down the back of the settee before going to the off-licence then none of this would have happened and there would have been no dust to settle and everyone could have gone back to their normal lives and no one would have been any the wiser.

And a few weeks later, when all the dust had settled, Darren Molloy Pearson's was a decent enough funeral, all things considered. There was a drive past the front gates even though he hadn't worked for Samson Brothers, though only because that was the only way to get from Acomb Street to the Welston Old Road. Nevertheless, there were a couple of people outside to watch the procession go by. Albert and Alma Green from the Purchasing Department, had known Darren Senior from a little boy, a cheeky young urchin with short cropped blond hair and plasters on his knees.

But all that was still to come, and back in the car park Simon Standage was still in the process of making a right pig's ear of matters.

'Anyone caught standing by anyone else's desk, just standing and talking, will be sacked on the spot, immediately,' he screamed again through his hand-held megaphone.

Lorna Smith was next to him at the time and she couldn't believe what she was hearing.

'Is he mad or what?' she said, which was very unusual for Lorna Smith, who normally wouldn't say boo to a goose, even at the best of times.

Simon Standage, an office in the executive suite, six years out of law school, married with a little girl called Sadie and a detached house in Marple Bridge. And eight months into his new position of Assistant Personnel Director and five weeks after that tannoy message, which resulted in a total walk-out by the entire workforce and a strike that lasted for two weeks and which was only ended with a promise of a pay rise across the board, it was decided that promoting Simon Standage to the post of Assistant Personnel Director may perhaps have been a tad previous, even for such a bright young man, and maybe an indefinite spell as the Recycling Wastes Co-ordinator might just be more up his street. And if truth be known it was quite a relief for Simon. His hair was getting thin, the stomach cramps had got worse and surely would have turned into ulcers by now.. And at nights they would finish off at least two bottles of Liebfraumilch with every evening meal and think nothing of it. Now at least he had the time to think and reconsider his situation overall. Maybe Jane had a point. There was nothing left for him here. And with those redundancies coming up, well, they'd had the idea for a long time now – to own and run a vegetarian café in the middle of the town centre.

six

And then there was all the mopping up to do, which was Lorna Smith's job on that particular Wednesday, as mopping up was done by rota to make things fair. The roster would be posted on the noticeboard at least two weeks ahead so as not to cause any arguments in case someone had to drop out. Naturally there was the usual swopping of days. Only last week Mary had asked to swop her Tuesday for Lorna's Thursday because her son had fallen off his motorbike and had been rushed to St Clare's Accident and Emergency. Lorna told Mary not to worry about doing her Thursday as well.

'You've enough on your plate, love. They say that music is good for a coma. He's into heavy metal music, your Steven, isn't he, if you can call it music? Still, what does it matter, eh? It's a start at least. If you run out of records I can always get our Frank to put a tape together. He's potty about heavy metal too. Drives me mad but still, if it keeps him happy.'

If only she'd known there'd be a fire alarm evacuation then she would have done something about it like phone in sick. But that was the trouble with these fire alarms.

'Talk about catching you off guard. The thought of those mucky feet all over my nice clean floor. Makes me wanna cry it does.'

Lorna Smith, twenty-seven years old, married to Frank for eight years, two children, Sally and Mark. There would have been three, only the one after Sally and Mark had miscarried. Lorna was in the middle of cooking the Sunday lunch when all of a sudden she didn't feel too good.

'So I thought I'd book an appointment with the doctor the next day, thinking it was nothing more than just a little leakage, you know. I'd had two already so it was nothing out of the ordinary. Or so I thought. They kept me overnight, for observation. Precautions, the nurse said. Just to make sure, which was fair enough really, but still. Apart from that, what can I say? Frank was more upset than I was. Don't get me wrong. I'm not saying I wasn't sad but as Elaine, one of the nurses said, *Hey, it's a right messy business being a woman,* and she's right too. It *is* a right messy business.'

Lorna Smith, married and two kids. Was never one for words. Actions spoke louder as far as she was concerned, and if it was up to her no way should she be working at a place like this.

'Are you mad? I'd be staying at home and looking after the kids, no messing. Hey, don't get me wrong. Frank's a good man, he does his best. And no complaints in the bedroom department neither, well no more than everyone else has. I mean, let's be frank, if it's not one thing with men its the other, and besides, all the overtime God sends he does but you know how it is nowadays. Even if I wanted to stay home we couldn't afford it. It all mounts up, don't it: Sally's school uniform, not to mention school dinners, games kit and school trips on top of all that. And the palaver when it's school holidays or when one of the kids is off sick, good grief, I'm telling you. It's not like on the telly any more, you know, them old black and white films where the women stayed at home all day wearing aprons with the sleeves rolled up, having gossips at the top of the street about you-know-who doing you-know-what with whoever was available at the time, sending little Jimmy to the corner shop for a loaf for your dad's tea in case he gets mithered when there's nowt on t'table and puts the belt to you. And on a Wednesday afternoon it's down to the washhouse down the road with the week's washing in the babby's old pram and you're there with the rest of the mothers and daughters and you'd be scrubbing away in the same basin you use every week with a scrubbing brush, a bar of carbolic and a Baby Blue, and you have a sing-song with the rest of the girls, and there's even some of you who can talk to each other above the din of the machines by using lip-reading skills which they picked up at the Ashworths' Cotton Mill before they closed it down. Stay at home and be a housewife? Chance would be a fine thing.'

seven

Not that any of this talk of husbands and children was any concern of Margery Watkins or Trish Yates last Friday night. Friday night was party night at the Quavers Discotheque on the Bardsley Road – music by Hamilton Bohannon, Earth Wind and Fire, anything really, even Disco Duck. So long as it made you get to your feet to groove your funky stuff – feet don't fail me now. Quavers Discotheque on Bardsley Road just by the reservoir where Margery's dad went fishing as a kid. Every Friday night, religiously like, with Trish Yates, yes that Trish Yates, PA to Cameron Taylor, Sales Director for Home Sales, though you'd never believe it at times. A bit of a one was Trish Yates. Calls a spade a spade right to their face and sod the consequences – *I speak as I find*. Friday night was party night at Quavers Discotheque – a couple of Pernod and oranges at the Sawyers Arms beforehand, then a five-minute taxi ride direct to the front door. And now the dance floor was chock-a-block to the rafters, it was that kind of record – feet don't fail me now.

And the last thing Trish needed was Margery whingeing on about that Clive Barnes and bleeding work. For goodness sake, Marg, give us a break . . .

'Don't get me wrong,' said Trish. 'You're me best friend and all, and I love you to bits, but sometimes you really get on my tits. Tell him to stick the sodding job where the sun don't shine. And failing that then up his arse. Talking of arses, look at the arse on that one, to your left, no *your* left.'

'Oh for heaven's sake, Trish . . .'

'Don't *Trish* me. You're a Section Head for fuck's sake and he's not. It's Clive Barnes we're talking about, remember? Dick for brains? I'd have chinned the bugger meself by now. Ginger-haired cunt. Bet his pubes are ginger.'

'Trisher Yates!'

Not that Margery minded that much. You knew where you stood with Trisher, which was more than you could say for some. And if the air became a little blue at times, then hey, what the hell. What was she always saying? *Take me as you find*. Even so, there was a limit – Trisher Yates!

'You've got to be kidding, I can smell his aftershave from here.'

'Okay, okay, don't wet yourself, Marg. So when is this job due in by?'

'Next Wednesday, no Thursday. They said they'd phone. All they want is a number and a date, that's all. I could throttle that Clive sometimes.'

'Bugger me, Marg. Is that all? Get the drinks in. I'll sort you out afterwards.'

Margery rolled her eyes. 'For goodness sake, Trish. You're joking, aren't you? I mean, look at him. What's that on his face. Oh yes, bum fluff.'

'Oh belt up, woman, I'll be done by the time you get back, I always am.'

'You'd better be or else. The usual then?'

'A shandy bass. In a ladies' glass.'

According to Margery, it all began that Tuesday afternoon when Margery asked Clive to issue a new WI number for the job she was doing and Clive told Margery what she could do, and in no uncertain terms, and that nothing had changed from this morning, or yesterday, or the week before that.

'Not without a signed facsimile of the original sheet, counter-signed and dated by a Unit Head,' said Clive at the time.

'Soddin' hell, Clive,' said Margery, 'you didn't say that the last time.'

'Then you'll remember me saying it can't be done, won't you?'

'Oh Clive, all it takes is your say so and that's it, *you* know that.'

'It's more than my job's worth and *you* know that.'

And now, a week later from the last confrontation with Clive, as far as Margery was concerned, she was going to do exactly as Trish said last Friday at Quavers Disco on the Bardsley Road – music by Hamilton Bohannon, Earth Wind and Fire, anything really, even Disco Duck. So long as it made you get to your feet to groove your funky stuff – feet don't fail me now. And according to Trish, the stockroom at the end of the corridor was full of shelves of old Lever Arch files from the days when Adam was a lad. Not that Clive knew any of this at the time. Not that he would have done much about it even if he had. With Margery being best mates with Trish Yates and all, Trish Yates, mouth almighty and tits to match.

eight

Henry's Makeup Tips 2
Eyes
by Henry Johnson

Introduction

When I first started, my goodness, I was doing it all wrong for years. I'd just glob on the eyeliner like there was no tomorrow and slap on the shadow straight afterwards – the mess, I'm telling you. Imagine Barbara Cartland after a night on the razzle. So I started reading magazines, studying women I saw, and most of all practising whenever I had the chance. It's like any other craft really, any other hobby. Practice makes perfect.

There are many rules of thumb that say to do eyeshadow before eyeliner. There are good reasons for this because you tend to put on less and the line appears smoother. However, I'm terrible with eyeliner so I put it on first because if I make a mistake I can wipe it all off and start again.

Eyeliner

Eyeliner can make or break you. I would recommend you avoid liquid eyeliner. The last time I used one of those, oh brother – not that the eyeliner was the problem, oh no, they test them on baboons and cats long before any humans try them. No, I was leaning on the chair trying to give meself a better angle to put the stuff on, only I leant back too far and the next thing I knew I was in St Luke's Accident and Emergency having me head bandaged after twenty stitches. Good job me wife had her yoga classes cancelled on account of the teacher being off sick with a pinched vertebra or else I'd have been there for ages. Even so, the mess on the carpet, I'm telling you, no amount of scrubbing would budge the stuff, we had to buy a new one in the end. Anyway, all that's beside the point – use an eye pencil instead, preferably one with a soft tip.

(1) First, decide on the look you're going for, e.g. daytime, career girl, night-time, slut. Once you decide this you can begin. For daytime or career girl you want to use a light touch. For night-time or slut you can use a thicker line. I suggest starting off with a little then adding more until you've got what you want.

(2) Do not line the inside of your eyelid. Not only is this unsanitary and prone to cause eye infection, it will also make your eyes look small and withdrawn.

(3) For career girl/daytime, take your pencil and point to your pupil, making the pencil vertical and parallel to your face. Now look at where the pencil crosses the lower lid. This is where your lower line starts, and you take it out to the outer edge of your eye. I usually start with my right eye. If you're left-handed, follow the same technique but use the left eye as a start. Take your left hand and stretch your right upper eyelid outwards so that your eye closes and the eyelashes point downward. Now you have a straight line to draw on. Take your pencil and make a line from end to end. Then all you have to do is smudge and shape. For night-time/slut, follow the same procedure only draw a thicker line, arcing upwards, so giving you more of an area to smudge and shape. Or in other words, a little less for career girl/daytime, a little more for night-time/slut.

You can also experiment with more colourful eyeliners, though I would not recommend this if you are trying to pass in public. Stylish or faddish techniques will only attract attention. But if it's attention you want, well, be my guest. Only have a decent pair of running shoes handy, you'll need them.

Eyeshadow

Eyeshadow is just that – *shadow*. Use it subtly to accentuate the eyes. Do not draw attention to your shadow but rather use it to accent the positive features of your eye shape. Buy a box of complementary shades. *Eyeshadow Trio* it's called, I think, something stupid like that – ludicrous name if you ask me, you'd think they'd come up with something better with the money they're on – hey, don't get me started.

(1) Take the lightest colour and cover the whole area below your brow and your upper lid. Sometimes I dab a little foundation on first before applying shadow to make it last longer. Once you've covered both upper portions, go ahead and sweep underneath your lower lid.

(2) Next take the medium shade and shade your eyelid.

(3) Take the darkest shade and make an arrowhead shape on the outer edge of your eye, yes, like so.

(4) Take the darkest colour and with the point of the applicator line the crease where your lid meets your eyebrow temple. Now smudge and blend. This is very important. All the colours should gradually and subtly shade into each other.

Conclusion

Okay, that's my method for eyes. Always remember that *less* is *more* when it comes to makeup. Also, do not concentrate too closely on one area. The important effect is the whole face. Subtleties can, however, make a huge difference to the overall look. Use the techniques above and with a little practice you'll get the look for you.

Good luck – and remember, practice makes perfect.

nine

Even Matt had to admit that Clive Barnes was the last person he would have expected to have gone berserk with a hammer in the middle of the new B&Q superstore on the Snide Estate off the Welston Old Road. Not that it made a whole lot of difference in the end. Whichever way you looked at it, what Clive got up to at the new B&Q on the Snide Estate off the Welston Old Road on a sunny Sunday afternoon was his business and nobody else's, and if it had been up to Clive then the whole thing would have been kept quiet and nobody would have been any the wiser. Besides, what the hell was Matt doing there anyway? Matt's Sunday afternoons were sacred: the car boot sale flea market in the meat bay of Cornfield Market – £6 per car, every Sunday come rain or shine, so what the hell was he doing at B&Q? Still, the cat was out of the bag and what's done is done, after yesterday's events at 2.15pm or thereabouts. It was hard to tell the exact time from under a pile of tins of Dulux emulsion.

The whole of the first floor would know by now, and by clocking-off time it would be all over the factory as well as the offices, even the medical centre which was half a mile down the road; maybe even in that night's edition of the *Manchester Evening News*. Hopefully the whole messy episode would have run its course by Christmas, but until then there was no use in hiding. At 10.30 on a Monday, it was still early days, and as Clive well knew from bitter experience it was best just to play along until something else more interesting turned up, like an earthquake or a stampede of buffaloes, or even better, the Queen dropping dead because of a heart attack.

'Besides,' said Clive, 'you should see the bruises down me left-hand side. You can have a look if you like.'

'No thanks, love,' said Irene, 'I've just had me breakfast.'

'You sure?'

'Yes I'm quite sure dear, thank you very much.'

'You sure it was Clive?' said Henry to Matt, earlier that morning at about 8.05, which Henry remembered because it was unusual for Matt to arrive on time.

'Of course it were Clive,' said Matt. 'I'd recognise that ginger hair from a mile off. I'd have offered to help only I was with the wife. Besides, the ambulance was on its way by then.'

'Ambulance? You said nothing about no ambulance,' said Henry, even more worried now.

'Give us a break,' said Matt, 'I ain't even had chance to take me coat off yet.'

Nevertheless, it was quite a relief for Henry when Clive came through the office doors later that morning.

'Must have been quite a mess,' said Henry.

'It was only the one can of paint. Good grief, that Matt can exaggerate at times,' said Clive, though even he had to admit that Matt was spot on with the other bits. Like the ambulance, the broken glass and the rolls of Anaglypta wallpaper strewn all over the place. Not that Clive had any recollection of this at the time, seeing as he had been having his first epileptic fit in twenty years, or so he'd told the police and the medics afterwards. Back then the doctor had advised his parents these things could go either way, even with treatment.

'He could grow out of them, or maybe not, one can never tell.' Clive had been about eleven or twelve, so in some ways it could be said that he had been very fortunate to have gone this long, almost twenty years in fact, though now, at 10.30 on a Monday morning and with all this talk, it was difficult for Clive to see the up side to anything.

'Our Maureen had been on at me for ages for one of those conservatories like the one in the brochure, you know what our Maureen's like when she gets a bee in her bonnet,' said Clive after giving Henry a blow by blow account of yesterday's incident at B&Q, or at least an edited version, from what he could remember, which wasn't much actually if truth be known, but even so, £2.50 for a can of woodstain?

'Yes, that's what I said,' said Clive. 'Two-pound-fifty for a two-pint tin.'

'Two-pound-fifty? Daylight robbery,' said Henry. 'Mittons do it for a pound.'

'Yeah, but that's a pint. The Mittons off Derby Street, by the traffic lights?'

'A pint, a litre, same thing. Both ways you were robbed blind.'

'Yeah right, Henry, if you say so.'

'And I do say so,' said Henry, still relieved to see Clive come in this morning. So much so that maybe now *was* a good time to say, yes Clive, you can go to Holme Lodge as my replacement like you've been asking all along. No, don't thank me, it was nothing. Hey, don't you worry about Reg Prentice, I'll sort him out. Besides, what Reg don't know won't hurt him.

Not that seeing Clive arrive that morning was the only thing Henry had had cause to be relieved about lately. To think it was only Wednesday last week when he thought his whole world had collapsed, or his Thursday evenings at least. When *that memo* first appeared on his desk. The memo itself left no room for any misunderstanding, with the important points in bold letters.

> **Thursday and Friday 26–27 April, Development Conference at Holme Lodge** (which was somewhere in the middle of the Oxfordshire countryside).
> **Compulsory for anyone over the grade of Unit Head or E3, or by special invitation.**

Which included Henry, of course, being the Unit Head of Technical Support, even though it was only a two-man unit, him and Clive. And also Reg Prentice, being the overall Department Head and all, which included the Contracts Unit, Overseas Sales and the Typing Pool on the second floor. So it went without saying that Reg should also have been down to attend the meeting. Only Reg had done his usual stunt and wangled his way out of going. The usual kind of excuse, copper-plated, safe as houses and as good as a sick note from the Pope knowing Reg. Which was fine by Henry, only it didn't help his situation, not in the slightest.

'Thursdays are sacrosanct, Reg, you know that,' said Henry. 'Blood and sands, Reg, it's Thursday nights, blood and sands, Reg, blood and sands.'

And of course it went without saying that Reg had not the slightest intention of asking what the hell Henry got up to on a Thursday night to make it so sacrosanct as he knew already. Everyone and the vicar's cat knew. Henry's Thursday nights had been common knowledge for a long time now. And if being kitted out like Vera Lynn made him happy then who was anyone to argue. Each man to their own as they say round these here parts, so long as the net curtains were kept drawn. Still, none of this changed the situation and under no circumstances could exceptions be made.

'You know as well as I do, Henry, it's a three-line whip. My hands are tied and that's all there is to it. And that reminds me. On the way home past Tescos tonight. Whipped cream.'

And now matters had been sorted, perhaps a change of subject wouldn't go amiss.

'Mutt and Jeff, eh,' said Reg. 'Damn Yanks. Everywhere you look. I was right in the middle of cutting the hedges when out they popped from behind the neighbours' leylandii – I've been at them for ages to cut the damn thing down, cuts out the sunlight and everything – anyway, there they were the both of them and they ask me about that interim report on the proposal to convert the Higher Maltby site into a theme park similar to the one at Alton Towers. Which I hadn't a clue about, of course. Still, it didn't stop the wife inviting them in for tea and biscuits despite my dirty looks. Which was just typical of her. Ever since I forgot to pick her up from aerobics class twice. There's only so many times you can say sorry but oh no, not our Mavis. Not one to let things drop is our Mavis. And while I have your attention, here's a tip for all you gardeners out there. You've been out in the garden all day and your hands are filthy but the last thing you want is dry hands from using too much soap. Here's a tip on how to keep them nice and soft: hot water of course, and any kitchen soap or washing-up liquid and sugar, yes sugar, about two tablespoons should do it. A vigorous scrub under the hot tap, great for clearing bits of dirt from under your fingernails. Not only does the dirt fly off, it also keeps the hands and fingers soft and supple, I swear by it myself.'

Later on that Monday evening in the hospital ward at St Luke's Infirmary, it had been a close run thing. If Clive hadn't left work right away as soon as he felt the nausea coming on and driven straight back to the hospital then

God knows what would have happened. He was in a bed near the telly, a bit of a nuisance really, especially when the channels needed changing and the remote control had been missing for over a month now.

'I wouldn't mind,' said Clive to Maureen during visiting hours that evening, 'only the nurses just sit on their backsides doing nothing all day but bed-baths when you don't want them.'

It had been over four hours since Maureen had got the urgent message to go to St Luke's to see her husband who had made his own way to the hospital. Not that she was surprised. She'd tried to tell him, suggested having time off sick, two weeks perhaps, even three, a note from the doctor, do him the world of good. Or even take the remainder of the holidays that were due to him. She'd almost said might as well, it's not like you'll be needing them, but she caught herself just in time. She'd even suggested that he told someone at work. Henry perhaps. Tell him everything, the whole shooting match, then he could pass it on to the others in his own time, in his own way, which would be more than all right knowing Henry, he was good like that was Henry. But then, as usual, nothing came of it, which was typical of Clive, terminal illness or not. Talk till you were blue in the face. Still, Clive was in good voice so that was something at least.

'I could not believe my ears,' said Clive. 'That Margery Watkins, talk about barefaced cheek. The gall of the woman. Who the hell does she think she is?'

And Maureen sat there and listened, trying hard not to

sigh. Visiting time would be over in ten minutes so all she had to do was nod and agree, and say anything she liked, he wasn't taking a blind bit of notice.

'Yes dear, no dear, anything you say dear, the dinner's in the dog dear.'

Besides, it gave her time to think of other things, other more important things. The doctor had advised her that the end could be any time and could come without warning, you could never tell with these things. Weeks, months, years perhaps. Any time any place anywhere. Any time any place anywhere. Now where had she heard that before. Oh yes, an advert on the telly from way back.

ten

Even Irene was at a loss to explain her sudden outburst. Wednesdays were Dean's football nights with the lads so it wasn't like there was anything out of the ordinary. It wasn't like she had nothing to occupy her either. Wednesday nights meant *Coronation Street* or a wildlife documentary on BBC2. Nor was it the time of the month either. Those days were long past now and good riddance to bad rubbish, but even so.

'You men,' said Irene, 'you're all the same. You sit there and you moan that the world's against you and everything but you do bugger all about it. And leave that remote alone, I'm trying to watch *Emmerdale Farm*. Go off to your silly football, see if I care.'

And the following evening in the Sailor's Arms, when all the fuss had died down, Dean was still scratching his head, trying to figure out exactly what had set Irene off, and trying to explain to his mates the events of last night – why he'd spent the whole night with Irene in his arms, cradling her, soothing her like a baby, instead of meeting up with the team van as arranged outside the rugby club at 7.30 sharp.

It had been the semi-final as well, the Arthur Mason Memorial Cup. Their very first semi-final, the biggest game in their history. Unless they won and reached the final, which they did of course, two-one, no thanks to Dean.

'Come on, lads,' said Dean. 'I couldn't just leave her like that, you'd have done the same, you would have.'

Which didn't go down at all well with the rest of them, lads being lads of course. That was the price you had to pay when you lived with a woman more than old enough to be your mother, though no one was about to say as much, not to Dean's face anyway.

'And on top of all that she ruined a good shirt as well. Armani, twelve-ninety-nine from the Arndale Centre.'

Still, a win's a win and the semi-final as well, the winner being in injury time, scored by Tom the goalkeeper of all people. Dean was sure they were taking the piss.

'What the hell was he doing up there in the first place,' said Dean. If it had been Mark or Trev then it wouldn't have been so bad really, but Tom? Tom the fat bastard, the fat bastard, nice enough bloke, nice car, Volvo 340 GL, but a fat bastard all the same.

And the others laughed, seeing as he had just bought the last round. No point in staying on his good side now, which was fine by Dean. He wasn't about to let on about not caring less about a football match, even though it was the semi-final, the biggest game in their history. If only the lads knew. But then they wouldn't be lads, would they, because lads weren't supposed to know about caring, crying throughout *The Color Purple*, doing umpteen things at once without making a mistake and not asking for thanks.

Still, Dean could talk the talk like everyone else. He could be gutted as the next guy, sick as a parrot, on the surface at least. In the meantime, he'd better keep his own thoughts to himself.

'What do you mean you were bored, for fuck's sake, you're the goalie, Tom, you're meant to be bored.'

She needed me and that was all there was to it. No questions asked. Semi-final or not. The biggest match in our history? Bugger that for a game of soldiers. For Pete's sake, Dean, you've a pub across the road, a curry house and a kebab shop within spitting distance, a season ticket for Maine Road, sex every other night and *she's got big tits, video and TV with remote control, your Ford Capri has just passed its MOT – you'll be wanting jam on it next.*

'What if they'd broken away and scored? Hey lads, don't laugh, I'm serious, for fuck's sake. I'll chin someone in a minute.'

Not when she needed me like that. It felt good to be needed. You can't buy that feeling, not like you can buy aftershave or a brand-new car. Being there because she wanted me. Yes, it felt really good. Just holding her like that, with her head on my shoulders and the both of us curled up, all snug and comfy cozy like. A cup of camomile tea whenever she wanted – one saccharin, no sugar, that's right, chuck, isn't it? How much do you love me? A pound of sugar. A pound of sugar? For Pete's sake.

'They would have had an open goal at least and there was no guarantee you'd get back in time. I mean it, what the hell were you playing at? Don't get sarky with me. No, I don't want a drink, sit down, I ain't finished.'

Whenever she's ready. In her own good time. Whatever was mithering her and all. In her own good time. I'll be here as long as it takes. Football, eh? Bugger that. You can't have everything, can you? If she didn't want to say then it was fine. Where does it start, eh? Where does that old slippery slope begin, where one minute you're sat watching football on the telly with the lads, the next you're in the video shop and you're hiring out The Sound of Music *and instead of two cans of Carlsberg Special and a plate of bacon butties it's a bag of toffee-coated popcorn for Irene and a bag of Maltesers for yourself and a large bottle of one-calorie Diet Pepsi between the both of you, with cups of course, and with a bit of luck the phone won't ring more than three times while the tape's playing.*

'You're the bleeding goalkeeper for fuck's sake, hey lads, don't laugh, I said already, it's not funny.'

eleven

'You must have seen it, Irene, they always repeat it on the telly, hundreds if not thousands, I bet. That missed goal from Pelé, what do you mean, who's Pelé? That Brazilian footballer from the World Cup, the 1970 World Cup. I was at school at the time. Anyway, that miss of his, much much better than any goal you'll ever see in your life, take my word for it. Of course you haven't seen it, you couldn't have or else you'd know what I mean, anyway, it's against Czechoslovakia or one of them communist countries, there's a long pass from the midfield to just outside the penalty area, and Pelé, he sees a defender coming towards him, only instead of running to catch the ball, this Pelé he does the opposite right, he runs away from the ball, see, the ball goes right and Pelé goes left, well actually he runs in an arc, like, a curve, and that's what confuses the player because he follows Pelé and forgets to follow the ball, which is the genius of it when you think about it, tricking the defender to follow him instead of the ball, which is bloody brilliance whichever way you look at it, don't you agree? Forget Einstein when it comes to genius, Pelé's the one in my book. What do you mean, is that it? Are you mad, that's not even the half of it neither. The best is yet to come, I almost wet meself just thinking about it. No, Irene, I'm okay, I went five minutes ago, just a figure of speech. Anyway, where was I? Like I said, he runs in an arc, like, so by the time he's done the arc he actually meets up with the ball again, only this time he's taken out two defenders, yes, two defenders, like I said, bloody brilliant, and not only that, the goalie's running after him like a ton of bricks, and this is the best bit, I'm coming to the best bit right now . . . No, Irene, England won it in 1966, me first year in secondary that year, secondary modern not grammar, I never passed me eleven-plus, I said already, haven't I? Anyway, this Pelé, he has the ball now in the penalty area to the far right as you watch it on the telly – how could I see it live, it were in Mexico for goodness sake, I mean, we only had black and white telly in them days, and not even BBC2 neither. Where was I up to? Ah yes, this Pelé, only now he's got his back to the goal and he's got the goalie and them two defenders I mentioned running after him like they want to break his legs, why, because he made them look a right bunch of wallies, I'm telling you. So this Pelé, he's facing the wrong way to goal, the goalie and two defenders are bearing down on him and David Coleman's doing the commentating, God I hate that David Coleman, him that does *Sportnight with Coleman*, see you've heard of him so you'll know what I mean. So Pelé, he swivels his hips and shoots, yes, he shoots, and the ball, it goes past the defenders, past the goalie's outstretched arms then it flies past the far left post and misses by inches, yes inches, yes that's what I said, it missed, the far left post, yes, as opposed to the left-hand post on the left-hand side, yes, where Pelé was in the first place, yes, when you watch it on the telly – not forgetting the goalie – yes you're right, and the two defenders, what do you mean it can't be any good if it missed, have you been listening to a word I've been saying?'

Ideally Irene would have liked to have stayed a little longer, as a favour to Henry – *No problem, Henry, sure I'll keep an eye on Clive, poor thing, while you're with Reg in his office, it's the least I can do, anything to help, poor thing* – but she was up to her eyeballs in typing and photocopying and God knows what.

'Very nice, dear. Pelé, yes, I remember him now, played for Brazil, dark-looking fella, like that Sidney Poitier . . . Oh is that the time? Sorry dear, got to go, I've a five-thousand-word file to type up before lunchtime or else Reg will play blue murder.'

And with that she was out of the office like a shot. She'd done all she could but there was only so much time in the day. At this rate it would be unpaid overtime, yet again.

As for Reg, he couldn't give a monkey's one way or the other. Pelé, Geoff Hurst or even Gordon Banks. It would be setting a precedent, and there were no two ways about it.

'Hey, if it was left up to me, Henry, I'd let him go. Clive's a nice lad and all, how's his wife anyway, are they still trying for kids? No, given up have they, a shame that, but still, if it wasn't meant to be then that's it, isn't it? Like I said, Henry, Clive's a good sort but I don't care if he's had his heart set on going, he ain't, and that's final. He just ain't senior enough. Section Head or above, you know that. We ain't social services you know, we can't give in to everyone who has their heart set on something. Besides, you know what they're like round here, you let one go and they'll all be clamouring to, for Christ's sake. Henry, it would be setting a precedent and you know me when it comes to precedents, I would have thought it would have been common knowledge by now.'

Meanwhile, back in the office, Irene had long since given up and left, which was just as well as Clive was past caring by now. Not that he had been alone for long, mind you. It was about a minute after Irene had run out of the office doors when suddenly, like a vision out of nowhere, there they were, right in front of him. The two American executives, on an eighteen-month secondment. Offices at the end of the director's suite on the ground floor. Others had spoken of having similar experiences: one minute you were talking and minding your own business, the next minute the two of them would appear just like that from out of nowhere. Mutt and Jeff, Mutt on the left and Jeff on the right, always. Not their real names, of course, but so long as they weren't called that to their faces then it was harmless enough. And at least Jack Robins was off the critical list in intensive care, which was something at least. Not that all the blame could be laid at Mutt and Jeff's door. They weren't to know about Jack Robins' recurring angina problems, but when you tell a man that the job he's been doing for fifteen years, after five years' nights doing City and Guilds, is about to be terminated and replaced by a £21,000 robot bought second-hand from a lace manufacturer in County Antrim, Northern Ireland, then you deserve everything you get.

Mutt and Jeff. Mutt on the left, Jeff on the right. They could have been Mormons or Jehovah's Witnesses. A couple of bibles in their hands and rows of Barratt houses on a Sunday afternoon and they'd have been right at home.

Mutt, the one on the left, cleared his throat. 'The interim report?'

Clive was at a loss as to what he meant.

'WI 65948?'

Jeff piped in, 'WI 65948. Work instruction number 65948. Work instructions, A4 sheets with each stage of the component or apparatus assembly detailed step by step and the signature column at the far right for stamping or signing by the Unit Head of that particular section?'

'Yes,' said Clive, 'WI 65948, yeah that one, right.'

'Yes, that's the one,' said Mutt and Jeff in unison. 'Been on your desk for three weeks now. Three weeks, two days and four hours to be exact.'

Clive tried to clear his throat. The nauseous feeling and sensation of impending doom were still there, and the sight of those two smiling Yanks wasn't helping matters neither.

'Been on your desk for about three weeks now? We assume all is in hand and on schedule? There is nothing you want to tell us is there, Clive? Because if there is then feel free to come to us anytime.'

'It's all right,' said Clive, 'I'll be on top of things by next week.'

Mutt and Jeff looked at each other and smiled.

'That's good news, Clive, very good news indeed.'

Jeff put his hand on Clive's shoulder. 'It's okay Clive. We've had a word with those concerned and, how can I put this?'

Mutt piped in, 'Everything is in hand as you folks say here in the north-west of England, there's no need for an answer, not right away, for another month at least. That's fine by you, Clive, isn't it? Another month perhaps, if that's fine by you.'

'We're agreed then,' said Jeff. 'Another month.'

There was a spare seat by Clive. Mutt, the one on the left, sat down. Any other time and Clive would have been annoyed as hell and played up a right stink. But with a queasy stomach to contend with maybe it was best to let matters run their course. Besides, it was hard to tell who was doing the talking, Mutt or Jeff, they were that alike it was uncanny really.

'As I hope you know, Clive, we are very much on side, aren't we?

'Yes we are and we want to support you every step of the way.

'If you find that our suggestions are not helpful—'

'Or that we are asking too much of you and decide that you would prefer to take another course of action then this would also be fine.'

'It's your decision in the end.'

'As I hope you know, we were extremely delighted to have the chance to work closely with you.

'We are very excited, very excited indeed, about you and the future of this here wonderful company of ours.'

'We cannot wait to see how things are going to turn out. As you folks say in the north-west of England.'

'We are that excited – *like*.'

As far as Clive was concerned, he couldn't give a flying fig whether they were excited or not. Right now his head felt like a wet September Sunday in Stoke-on-Trent, with a stomach to match. Maureen was right. He needed more than a couple of days off work. More like a week or a month or even a year – or longer? Maureen had warned him it would be like this. About a week ago, after the incident at B&Q.

'You might as well tell 'em, love. They'll know about it soon enough. What if the worst thing happens right in the middle of a job. What then, eh? Listen, love, it's not fair to the others, put yourself in their shoes. It's not easy for me either, you know. Waiting for a phone call, you know, waiting for the worst. Trust me, in some ways you have it the easiest. Yes, I know what I'm saying but why bother, eh? Talk till I'm blue in the face.'

But that was a week ago, and a lot of water had passed under the bridge since then. And Mutt and Jeff were well into the groove by now.

'Now, *Our* Clive, you don't mind me calling you *Our* Clive? You see, *Our* Clive, we understand how these things turn out but who are we to judge? As they say, to err is human –'

'– and to forgive is divine, wouldn't you say, *Our* Clive?'

It suddenly came to Clive what Mutt and Jeff reminded him of. A cartoon on the telly, one of those Warner Brothers ones, those who do Bugs Bunny and Elmer Fudd. The cartoon was about two mice – he couldn't recall their names – and they were living together in a tree. They talked to each other in clipped affected accents, using words like undoubtedly and indubitably, it was plain to see what kind of mice they were. And if you closed your eyes and switched the accent from English to southern American, Bob's your uncle, Mutt and Jeff. Uncanny really.

'I know what you're thinking, Clive. You're thinking there's no rhyme or reason to any of this.'

'Only to those who work here, of course.'

'And even then most have forgotten about them.'

'Or even why they were there in the first place.'

'And to what are we referring, I hear you ask?'

'Work instructions numbers of course, otherwise known as WIs. Work instructions, A4 sheets with each stage of the component or apparatus assembly detailed step by step and the signature column at the far right for stamping or signing by the Unit Head of that particular section. All of which you know, Clive, being the issuer of WI numbers for the whole department. A roll you inherited when the previous issuer for thirty-five years, George Street, retired five years ago.'

Mutt looked at Jeff, like he was asking for permission.

'Please, I've been practising with tapes for months, please.'

Jeff sighed. 'Oh, if you must, but try to keep it short.'

And Mutt continued to tell the story, but this time in a northern accent so good that if Clive had closed his eyes it could well have been anyone from down his street who was doing the talking.

'Yes, the same George Street who once retired found himself staying in and moping around the house until his wife got so fed up she threatened to stop baking his favourite steak and kidney pudding unless he found himself something to do. Which he did, lollipop man for the infants school round the corner. Eight to nine-thirty, three to four-thirty, every weekday, with his two uniforms and his own locker in the school basement. And he would have continued to do so if he hadn't got run over by an articulated lorry carrying export lager from Czechoslovakia, the driver having taken the wrong turning at the previous roundabout which was a mistake frequently made by anyone who didn't know the area very well. Obscure signs, you see, on account of over-grown sycamores. The locals had sent a petition to the council over a year ago now, but as is always the case it ended up on some official's desk at the back of beyond, might just as well have thrown it in the bin . . . Still, hasn't it turned out nice again, has it not?'

And just as suddenly as they had arrived, they'd gone. But not before Clive had told them a joke about an American warship and a Canadian lighthouse, which did not go down at all well if the looks on their faces were anything to go by.

twelve

Henry's Makeup Tips 3
Cheeks
by Henry Johnson

Introduction

First, the foundation, followed by the eyes and now the cheeks, yes, cheeks, the ones on your face, which ones did you think I meant? Right, that's it, playtime over. From now on, no funny bits, no more going off on tangents, I'm sticking right to the point. You just watch, philistines.

(1) Draw them

If you are like me and don't have prominent cheek bones then you will have to create an illusion through shadowing. The first step is to find your cheek bone and draw a line over it. Take a lipliner pencil, smile and start a single line where your cheek meets your nose, and continue it up towards the back of your face near your ear. Do this on both sides. I know this looks weird but trust me. Now smudge it so that it is not too defined.

(2) Dark contour

As with the eyeshadow, I use three shades of blusher – dark, medium, light. I usually start with a darker brown blush and shade right on the line, making it darker towards the hairline. Keep in mind that as with all make-up, less is more – repeat after me, less is more, less is more. Like a mantra – less is more, less is more, that's it. Now where was I? Oh yes . . . There's a lot more to come so you don't want it to jump out at you yet. This is just a shadowing technique.

(3) Jaw bone / chin / nose

That's right, the jaw bone – feel the bottom of your jaw bone and follow it back to where it meets your neck, like this, see? If you have a large face you may want to put some of the dark shadowing there. Remember, shadow conceals. Ditto with your chin – if you're cursed, as many of us are, with a double chin, shade there as well. If you have a wide nose you can thin it by shading the sides of your nose.

(4) Colour contour

Take the medium shade – the colour that you plan on wearing – and go over the same spot on your cheek bone. Remember – apply sparingly (less is more, less is more) and shade darker towards the back.

Oh, and while I remember, a little change of subject perhaps. Cardigans. I swear by them myself. An absolute godsend when I'm undecided what to wear. Whether you want to go the whole hog like Katie Boyle, or if you just want a Hilda Ogden/Ena Sharples slob out: a cheap frock, rolled up stockings, a cup of tea and a packet of woodbine, rounded off with a pair of comfy slippers. Well, believe you me, a decent cardy covers a multitude of sins. Wool, cotton, acrylic, so long as it feels comfortable next to the skin, I've a whole drawer of them. Marks and Spencer, the indoor market, Hitchens on the High Street across the road from the old magistrates courts, the one that does catalogue seconds. They know me there, think I'm buying for the wife. I don't wait for the wife to buy me one for special occasions or birthdays or the festive season neither. If I'm in the mood then it's out with the wallet. I mean, a cardigan's for life, not just for Christmas.

Now where was I? I've done colour contours so the next bit is, oh yes . . .

(5) Highlight

Take a lighter colour blush and follow the contour of your cheek.

(6) Tone it down

If you need to, take your pressed powder and go over your whole face again. You can never use too much pressed powder. This will make your face look soft and the colour in your cheeks natural. Just keep practising and you should be able to get it. Like I'm always saying, practice makes perfect.

th

White shirt and bright red braces. Thirty-five years old last Tuesday and married for six years, one boy and another child expected next May, a girl hopefully, fingers crossed. Paul Sinclair was on a roll. Clear overhead projections, colour slides in the right order, followed by a scale model to be wheeled in on a trolley when he gave the nod – he was *that* good – like shit off a shovel. He'd have won medals for it if they were handing them out.

Not in Harry White's eyes, mind you. Paul Sinclair was a lanky git who didn't know his arse from his elbow. Not that Harry's opinion counted for much these days. The writing had been on the wall and the whole place going to the dogs for a long time now and he should know. Harry was a local lad from round the corner, Addison Street. His dad had owned the grocer's shop by the corner, before it was sold and turned into a Chinese chip shop. At the last count it was thirty-five years industrial experience one way or the other, with three years off for National

…plenty back then. Engineering works …ace, you couldn't miss them there were that

'You could leave your job on a Friday and start a new one on the Monday, there were that many going back then, it was that easy.'

And now here he was, in a four-star hotel conference room in the middle of the Oxfordshire countryside. Harold Stanley White, Senior Procurement Manager for six years this November coming. Married thirty-two years this September. Four children, one daughter and three sons – Colin, thirty-one, a computer analyst, daughter Clare, twenty-nine, working in the media, Simon, twenty-three, a teaching student at Coventry Polytechnic, and language student Paul, eighteen. Three grandchildren and another one on the way, fingers crossed.

'Clare and her boyfriend Brian sometime in May. A girl they said. It's possible to tell nowadays. Those scanner devices like on the telly. They have the technology to do *owt* nowadays.'

Harold Stanley White. A founder member of the Rochdale Canal Society, who took part in the renovation of a derelict section of the Leeds-Liverpool canal at Littleborough, an honorary member of the Soroptimists, and survivor of a heart by-pass operation last year. It was only through Harry's persistent badgering that the plaque commemorating the dead from both world wars was finally put up on the factory gates. A big brass plaque with the names in alphabetical order, embossed in gold-plated italics. And where appropriate, the name of the medal won by the side: VCO, VC, DSO – those things meant a lot to folks back then.

Not that Harry had any complaints. He'd had his day, like the rest of his generation, so now was the time to put his feet up and leave the rest of it to the young uns. Harold Stanley White. Three years' National Service in Palestine just after the war. Most of it spent searching houses for weaponry, bombs or anyone suspected of being up to no good. Trenching up and down the desert sands checking for mines, four or five conscripts at a time. And if there was one thing that brought home to you how insignificant you were in the general scheme of things, it was having to traipse up and down in the middle of some bloody desert in the middle of the bleeding afternoon when the sun was at its hottest, where the only cover from some wog with a rifle was the flies and the sweat pouring down your face.

'Insignificant? Like a grain of sand, like a grain of sand. Still, I know a few folk round here could do with a dose of that, mentioning no names, Mister high and mighty red braces. Microprocessor silicon chips malarkey you get nowadays. Silicon chip this, silicon chip that, silicon chips with everything. Just call in some lanky-arse git with red braces and all is right with the world. Throw the baby out with the bath water while you're at it.'

'Talking to yourself again, Harry?' said Frank Clark, his opposite number for Home Sales. Only two years in this job, following fifteen years at Saltshafts down the road, but a Samson Brothers man all the same.

'Oh, sorry, Frank, forgot meself for a moment there. What's on the menu for dinner tonight?'

'A choice of fillet steak, pork escalopes or cod mornay if you're vegetarian. With crêpes Suzette for pudding.'

'Not quite pineapple chunks with condensed milk.'

'Hey up, Harry, you'll be wanting tripe next. Anyway, you've remembered that can of maggots like I asked, haven't you?'

'Yeah, they're in me jacket pocket. Don't see why though, I mean, you daft a'peth, the company's paying.'

'I know that but it's our twenty-fifth anniversary in a month's time and I've booked us a table at that Berni Inn on Trunk Street in the middle of town and I thought, well, why not get some practice in. I mean, it takes some planning it does to find maggots crawling about in your main course and cause enough fuss to get a full refund. So I thought, while we're here, what about a trial run?'

A week is certainly a very long time as they say in politics, and a week ago last Thursday, if anyone had said to Margery Watkins that she'd be at Holme Lodge with the rest of the suits she would have told them to pull the other one, pal. If it was up to Margery she'd much rather be spending Friday nights the same as usual at the Sawyers Arms with Trish before moving on by taxi to Quavers before ten-thirty. But Paul Sinclair had insisted. He'd even booked her train tickets. First class as well.

'You're the only one who knows anything about computers. It's worse than the dark ages here.'

And that was the end of the matter as far as Paul Sinclair was concerned, despite Margery's pleading that she wasn't allowed, being only a Section Head.

'I won't hear another word of it,' said Paul Sinclair. 'You're going and that's final. Besides, I don't need to tell you some radical changes are afoot around here, if you get my drift.'

Which just about summed it up really – Paul Sinclair was one of those people who prided themselves on having their fingers on the pulse at all times, but even he wasn't to know the exact details of the interim report on the future of Samson Brothers Site 1063, Higher Maltby division. He knew about the upheavals all right: the voluntary redundancies, a softener for the next round of redundancies, which would not be voluntary, of course, and would entail a reduction of the total workforce by fifty-five percent across the board over a period of two years, with several sections being phased out completely, to be followed by other sections over a period of time as the company deemed necessary. But even he wasn't to know the exact details of the interim report because basically the report had not been written yet and would not be completed for another six months at least. The authors were still on an eighteen month fact-finding mission at Higher Maltby, a year after completing their Harvard MBAs. Mark Digby and Richard T. Smith. Second and fifth of their class respectively, 1975. Not that they intended to make a song and dance of their stay in Higher Maltby. They'd even insisted on staying in local digs. Mrs Mason's board and lodgings on the Welston New Road next to Boots The Chemists. A ten-minute walk to the office every morning, past the junior school on Yale Street, past Reese Macdonald's Funeral Services, right up to the office gates.

All of which was intended to get a flavour of the place, a lay of the land so to speak. And according to the brief from head office, they had a free hand to do whatever was deemed necessary, wherever, to whomever – words to that effect. And with two months left of an eighteen-month contract, it had been decided between the both of them to spice things up a little, a few extra surprises here and there, whatever, wherever the moment arose, as they saw fit.

And this wasn't even the half of it neither.

It would have been difficult to know where to start really. The new M60 motorway ring road planned for the whole of Greater Manchester, due for completion in the year 2001. The multistorey car park on the site of the old K-Shed section. A brand-new shopping estate stretching from Acomb Street to Bacons Drive which would make the recently opened Snide shopping centre look like Legoland; as well as yet another Tesco hypermarket, the third one in Woodside, a Pizza Hut, a McDonald's of course – went without saying – something new from the States called Toys'R'Us, and on top of all that a massive multiplex cinema complex so big there were plans to have twenty-one screens at least, *yes, twenty-one screens*.

'Twenty-one screens? You're joking,' said Margery.

'I kid you not,' said Paul. 'You think that's bad, it ain't even the half of it neither.'

But all that was still way *way* off in the future, and as far as Margery was concerned, she was having a hard time taking any of this in, and maybe this was a good time to take a seat.

'I better sit down,' said Margery 'take the weight off me feet.'

Paul Sinclair pulled over a chair.

'I know, it's all a bit much to take in, isn't it?' said Paul Sinclair. 'Still, if anyone asks where you heard it from, you never heard it from me.'

But all that was a week ago to the day, in fact, and a week is a very long time, and now it was 4.30 pm Thursday evening, 26 April, by taxi from the station after a four-and-a-half-hour train journey from Manchester Piccadilly. As far as Margery was concerned, it wouldn't be much different from being back at Higher Maltby really. Far too many oversized egos and small dicks going around to get anything done properly. Only now they were all transported to four-star accommodation in the salubrious surroundings of the Oxfordshire countryside, which made a pleasant change at least.

And as for Clive Barnes, the look on his face.

'What the fuck are *you* doing here?' is what he really wanted to say, as Margery strode into the hotel foyer in her blue suit and skirt of sensible length, so as not to give anyone the wrong idea.

However, 'What a surprise seeing you here,' was the best he could muster, which was pretty good actually considering how much he'd had to bust a gut to get Henry to allow him to take his place here in the first place. Not to mention two days' extra unpaid overtime, a pint of Boddingtons every afternoon for two weeks, as well as unauthorised access to all the number codes in the WI file he kept in his desk. Now that last one really hurt. Clive might only be E2 but when it came to the issuing of WI numbers it made no difference whether you had an office on the executive suite or were invited for tea with the Queen. You had to come through him and no one else, Clive Barnes, City & Guilds, ONC, HND. And not without the appropriate signature from someone in authority or else you could whistle for it, *luv*. As Margery found out to her cost last week – the silly cow, who the hell did she think she was dealing with . . .?

'And now she's here, right here in front of me, in her blue suit with a skirt of sensible length,' is what Clive really wanted to say, though all he managed to get out about the suit was, 'Nice skirt.'

Not that Margery was all that thrilled to see Clive Barnes, but the company was paying and seeing as Paul Sinclair had insisted then who was she to argue? And besides, as her mother was always saying, if you can't say something nice then don't say nowt at all.

'Hello Clive, fancy seeing you here.'

And that did it as far as Clive was concerned; he was in no doubt whatsoever now. He hated Margery Watkins even more, so much so that he'd forgotten about the dizzy spells and nausea he'd had just five minutes ago. Just seeing her there like that, in her sensible shoes with sensible heels which set off her shapely ankles, her skirt which revealed just enough leg to suggest she worked out at the gym at least three times a week, a blue jacket and white blouse both sensibly buttoned up to reveal absolutely nothing to all but the discerning eye.

WELCOME TO HOLME LODGE
To the employees of Samson Brothers PLC
The Arkwright Suitc
Development meeting.
5.30 PM

on a black punched-hole board and in plastic letters that would not have looked out of place in a kindergarten playroom. The last thing anyone needed was a meeting at 5.30 pm, though strictly speaking it was still on company time. And as all those attending knew well enough, there were others back at Samson Brothers who would gladly take their place. The first meeting was meant to have been an ice-breaker, but Paul Sinclair had other ideas. He knew that they wouldn't be able to get back on the train fast enough when they realised what the meeting was about.

Still, long journey or not, at least Fred Bates was enjoying himself. What Fred didn't know about scales, key-sign issues and in-house time scaling you could fit on a postage stamp. Nor was he shy about letting anyone else know that. Anyone unlucky enough to be close by, as Margery was finding out now, to her cost. Not that there was much Margery could do about it. The seating had all been arranged. Some bright spark with red braces had decided that (for two days at least) position in the company didn't matter, you'd be seated as indicated on the noticeboard and you had to lump it. Not that Margery was against such democratic ideas, in principle, but when you were sat next to Fred Bates then principles were the first things out the window. Fred Bates, Mechanism

Designs. Groping Fred or Rambling Fred, depending on the time of day. She'd had a few close calls with him in the past. And now this. One consolation at least was being on the front row – plain view of the whole meeting. Which went some way to explain why he was rambling quite so compulsively. Even so, she almost wished he'd pinch her bottom or squeeze her tits and have it over and done with.

And as far as Donald Makin was concerned, compulsory seating arrangements or not, he was beggared if he was going to be sat next to that slimeball Dan Smith for the duration. It was bad enough having to face each other from their offices every single day, never mind having to share the same secretary. Not that he hadn't fought tooth and nail. But when it was explained to him in no uncertain terms that changes were afoot, which meant jobs had to go and if you wanted to keep your own secretary then it was fine by everyone though you might like to consider seriously, that no one was indispensable, nudge nudge wink wink, then there was not a lot one could do about it. But even so, *fucked* if he was going to stick to any *fucking* seating arrangements, *fucking* compulsory or not; if anyone wanted to make a *fucking* issue of it then let them, he'd had it up to *fucking* here with the *fucking* lot of them, *fuckers*, the lot.

Not that any of this mattered in the end to Paul Sinclair. Clear overhead projections, colour slides in the right order, followed by a scale model to be wheeled in on a trolley when he gave the nod – at this rate it was a foregone conclusion that he would be moving into the Technical

Director's office at the far end of the executive suite in the not too distant future. And Paul Sinclair was not about to be put off his stride, not by this lot. Not even by that pillock leaving the room right in the middle of his talk, without even a by your leave – the manners of some people. Someone said it was that Clive Barnes from Technical Support, but it couldn't be as everyone knew Henry Johnson was the Unit Head.

fourteen

The time, 8.45 am, Monday 5 August 1985; the place, Welston train station. It was usual for Wilma Marsh to take the train to work instead of the bus nowadays: £5.50 for a Zone 1 weekly pass to cover all her journeys. There were rumours of a further price increase, though, the second in six months. One of the many joys of working in Manchester Piccadilly.

Wilma Marsh. Personal Assistant to the Assistant Managing Director at the CDI off Ferrel Street. An extra three thousand pounds on what she was getting at Samson Brothers, all this and the redundancy package, well, who said a bad wind never blows.

Wilma wiped the condensation from the windows, trying to peer through. Trees, cars, buildings, the new shopping centre at Stafford Park where the old docks used to be, the usual stuff. She would always try to get a window seat. In the mornings that is, the evenings were a different matter altogether. Then you'd be so desperate to get a seat at all it didn't matter if it was next to a tramp or even Hughie Green. Wilma would always keep a packet of mint-fresh chewing gum handy just in case. And some wet-wipes, and a good book.

But still, Clive Barnes of all people, who'd have believed it, eh?

'Who'd have believed it, eh? Thirty-five years old he was – my age now. I was only talking to him that last Friday as well, he was in the office checking some figures for a job he was doing. I only remember it was Clive because of his ginger hair. And the swearing. Not that that was anything out of the ordinary for that lot. Just typical, effing this, effing that, whenever they can't find something they want, even though it was right there in front of him. I only had to turn a couple of the pages of the Lever Arch folder and there it was, the WI figures, exactly what he was looking for in the first place. Was there any thanks? Not on your nelly, but still, when I heard the news the next Monday, I was so relieved I hadn't given him a piece of my mind at the time like I'd meant to. I mean, I wouldn't have been able to live with meself.'

Wilma Marsh. Thirty-five years old. Personal Assistant to the Assistant Managing Director. School holidays were always the best for traffic, half-term, summer holidays and all that. Still, better that than those hapless mothers with their offspring on half-term attempting the weekly Tescos shopping with extra baggage. A fourteen-year-old daughter with raging hormones, a teenage son in desperate need of new trousers only he wouldn't be seen dead in C&A with his mother in case he bumped into his mates, the hyperactive six-year-old twin boys who might just as well be the bastard lovechildren of Lucifer himself.

'Yes, it's like most things really. Not being married, not having a family. Swings and roundabouts. At least the decorating's sorted.'

And if things went according to plan then the workmen would be done by the end of the month. The whole house decorated from top to bottom. Replastering, new electrics, all the walls wallpapered, even the toilets. Should add five thousand to the value of the house, at least. Not that Wilma had any intention of moving. Death, divorce and moving house, the three most stressful situations according to last month's *Cosmo*. And with death being inevitable anyway and the other one out of the question, then why give herself a hard time with all those removal men?

'Janice at work recommended the decorators. You can never be too sure nowadays, the cowboys going around calling themselves builders, frightening when you think about it.'

It went without saying that she could have saved a packet if she'd done all the work herself. It wasn't like she didn't have the time, after work and weekends, but for heaven's sake, she wasn't a man and she didn't want to be one either.

'Just to save three grand? Hardly seems worth it really. Pay someone to do it, that's what I say. Have a spare key cut, set some cups out for tea and coffee, and sugar and a packet of chocolate digestives – workmen tend to like chocolate digestives in my experience – leave the vacuum cleaner out in the open so they can't miss it. After that it's Bob's your uncle, apart from the wet paint and wallpaper drying a couple of days. Then sign the cheque, making sure the money's in the bank, take back the spare key, and have a good hoover down from top to bottom – you know what men are like when it comes to cleaning up – and that's it, a brand new house, well almost, at least five thousand added to its value. Money well spent if you ask me.'

Still, life was never that perfect, and if Wilma had had any say in the matter there would be a bus right from the top of the street where she lived which would take her directly to the office doors. Sixteen storeys high, 120 feet according to the company brochure, and officially the highest building in the whole of Greater Manchester, never mind Manchester Piccadilly. Yes, if it was up to Wilma. A bus right up to the office doors. One of those small red and white Morris buses. A single decker of course, a double decker would have no chance with some of those corners, especially the one near Daisy Nook as the road turns on to Welston Moss. And at 50p return weekdays – now that would be a perfect route.

'Chance would be a fine thing, still, God knows how long it had been since we'd spoken, me and Maureen, when I phoned her that Sunday. God knows how I remembered her phone number after so long: 362 5843. See, off the top of me head, after all these years, even though we've had it changed for the last six months since the move, you know for the life of me the new one slips me mind. It's always the case, isn't it? You have no problem remembering stuff donkey's years off but can you remember to take the steak and kidney pie out of the freezer for tonight's tea?

'I know we used to work in the same place but I'd have recognised Clive anywhere, with that ginger hair of his. Couldn't miss it. I'd only popped into B&Q for some bathroom tiles. Like I said, it were two years ago, I'd still had it in me head that I was a dab hand at DIY, you live and learn. Anyway, it was like a bomb had hit the place, stuff all over the shop, I'd have hated to be the cleaners afterwards. That ginger hair of his, a dead give-away, even with him sat squatted by the exit with his head in his hands. One of the staff was offering him a cup of tea at the time but he was having none of it. His eyes, they seemed so far away, like he was lost forever. I reckon the staff must have had training for that sort of emergency, you know, a lunatic going berserk with a hammer. I mean, one minute it's crash bang wallop, with the alarms going off and the whole of the kitchen section reduced to a pile of rubble; the next minute the tannoy's reassuring the shoppers that everything's under control, and the assistants have administered first aid, helped poor Clive to his feet and offered cups of tea to anyone who wanted one.

'Maureen filled me in with the exact details later on that night. She'd just that minute gotten in from the hospital. Thank heaven it was a Sunday and the traffic was clear. Of course I'd thought of going round to her house at the time but it had been so long, far too long. And anyway, I didn't know whether that Clive had done something terrible. I'm telling you, if you'd seen him that Sunday afternoon you'd have been thinking the same too. When she picked up the phone and answered, I'm telling you, I could have cried.

' "At Seventeen" by Janis Ian. A song in the charts, ages ago. We'd play it over and over again. Maureen's parents must've been sick to death of it, they never said nothing, though. They were good like that, Maureen's parents. Teenage girly nights in playing records and wearing makeup, that kind of thing. And when that Janis Ian song came out, well, it was written for us, wasn't it? At seventeen. That says it all doesn't it, at seventeen. Now look at us, the wrong side of thirty-three. Look at us, I said to Maureen, that time when I rang that Sunday evening for the first time in ages.

'They're only pop songs, she said, *just little pop songs.*

'You know something. I wish I'd gone round to see her that very afternoon like I'd had a mind to in the first place. It's always like that when you don't follow your first instincts. Not that it would have made any difference in the end but even so, when she said they're only pop songs just little pop songs, I could have cried.'

The time, 12.45 pm, Monday 2 April 1987; the place, Platform 5, Manchester Piccadilly railway station.

As far as Trish Yates was concerned, the Manchester to Edinburgh Waverley train was bad enough as journeys went even at the best of times, but with a case of the cramps? Talking to yourself helped.

'About anything really. The weather, price of shares on

the stock market, Doris Day films. The trick is not to stop, to keep going, legs and fingers crossed – never mind the quality, feel the width. Anything really. Even about what to expect when the train arrives at Waverley station. Apart from that long walk from platform thirteen to the exit, a bit of a bind after a four-hour journey, especially carrying all that luggage. Saying that, I'm beggared if I'm catching a taxi, at those prices you must be joking. There's a number ten bus just outside Boots on Princes Street which takes you straight to the students' residence, well there was one the last time I was up there.'

The 1.05 pm train, due to arrive at Edinburgh 4.35 pm, stopping at Preston, Berwick, Carlisle, Crewe at various stages and not in that order either, having originally set off from Penzance earlier that morning, 7.21 in fact, with its final stop at Aberdeen at 7.33 that evening, if everything went to plan.

'Personally, I couldn't give a toss one way or the other. Penzance, Bognor Regis, Timbuktu, who gives a toss? So long as I get there in one piece and there's a corner shop nearby to get me little nick nacks. I'll do a proper shop at the weekend, there's bound to be a supermarket near by, Kwik Save or Tesco maybe. And with a bit of luck I'll be in the bath by seven-thirty. A steaming hot Radox bath. I've a couple of sachets in the handbag. One of those promotions from *Cosmo*. I don't know how long, for heaven's sake, it's in me handbag isn't it, there's stuff in there from way back. Besides, I had to chuck some away me handbag were that full. That's the trouble with these long train journeys. You end up spouting all kinds of nonsense to yourself. Though it's not like there's anything else to do. The talent's not much to look at. The buffet coach is out of cheese and onion crisps and I've been to the loo three times already. The cramps, been bad with them all week. I said, didn't I? Nerves I expect. Toilet's been me second home these last few days. Thank heaven I bought a pack of wet-wipes. Last time I went the toilet was out of bog paper. No, I'm all right for the moment, thank you. So long as I keep talking I'll be fine.

'I'll ring Mum tomorrow, I'm fit to drop already and we've not even arrived yet. Saying all that, even now I still pinch meself at times. Me, little old Trish Yates, Edinburgh University, a degree in Pharmacy, a BSc, Bachelor of Science, and not the Polytechnic neither. The real Edinburgh University. The full Monty, like. Bet you're wondering aren't you. Trish Yates, BSc in Pharmacy, Edinburgh University, not the Polytechnic neither. Well, I don't mind talking, beats looking out the window anyroad. Keeps me mind off matters in hand. Oh God, oh fuck, oh thank goodness for that. For a minute there . . . No, I'm okay for now.

'Where shall I start? I always had me eye on one of those old universities anyhow, even before the redundancy money, like. It only took two years at the Tech, well it wasn't like it was the first time doing me A-levels, was it? Didn't I say? I went to the grammar school off Darnten Road, that one, yeah, before they turned it into a sixth-form college, you know, the one down Mabley Bridge. It were easier to get the train, flippin' 'eck, we'd have been late every day if we relied on the buses. Yeah,

Oxford, Cambridge, the like, the teachers thought so as well, until the fourth year mind you. Boys! I know what you're thinking. Trish Yates, anything in pants; Trish Yates, a gob on 'er like t'Mersey tunnel, secretary downstairs in the reception area, a shandy bass in a ladies' glass, well try this for size. *Carpe diem* – the Epicurean motto, you know, Seize the day! Or as they say round these parts, *You're a long time dead, chuck.*'

Keep talking Trish, keep talking.

'I'm telling you, it was surprisingly easy in the end. What did the guy on the phone say, the guy in Admissions, C and a D, that's what they asked for. On account of me being mature, like. *It is our intention to encourage as many mature students as possible,* which I thought was a bit of a cheek and I was just about to tell him as well but he must have seen the look on me face because then he went on to say it wasn't personal as anyone over the age of twenty-three was classified as a mature student. I said that's okay then, but still, for a moment back then I was ready to give him a right mouthful I'm telling you – what do you mean, how old am I? None of your business. That's for me to know and for you to find out. C and a D, that's what they asked for. On account of me being mature, like. Mind you, I got two As, in case they changed their minds. I wasn't taking no chances.

'Like I said, I'll be fine, so long as I keep talking.

'Margery, for fuck's sake, Margery, talk about sieve for brains. I'll phone her from the station. Oh my goodness. I was supposed to phone her last night. Oh well, it's a shame they don't have phones on trains, I can't believe I forgot. Trish Yates, sieve for brains or what. Not to worry, not like she'll be out anyway, I'll ring as soon as the train gets in. Four, five o'clock. She'll be in all right, unless she's asleep. Seven months is it now she said last time? She looks it too. Size of a horse. James wants another girl, Margery says. She says she's not bothered one way or the other so long as it's healthy. Which is fine of course if you're into that kind of thing. Saying that, I can't help but think it's a waste, him staying at home with the babby, like. I mean, he's got a degree and all. So what if she's a Unit Head? Margery swears blind it was his idea. She says he can't get enough of it. Already done up the spare bedroom as a nursery playroom, like. Yeah, I bet. Still, each to their own, I say, but even so, it's James who has the degree, not her. Don't get me wrong, women's lib and all that, that's me, but like I said to her on the phone the last time we spoke, you might be on more money being a Unit Head of Computing and Information Technology, but remember, any more redundancies and it could be you that's out on your ear. But what can you say? You know Marg when she's made her mind up. If anyone thinks I'll be staying at home looking after the kiddies once I've done me degree, they've got another think coming. I'll ring her tomorrow perhaps, or the day after, once I've sorted things out a bit more.

'I was told thinking about Cornflakes helps in this sort of situation, well not quite but near as dammit. A bloke I went out with a while back, forget his name. How did he say it again? Oh yes, when we had sex, he had this trick to stop him coming too soon. He'd think of Cornflakes, he said, just a plain bowl of Cornflakes. Without the milk, you can't take no chances, he said. Works a treat, he said, not that I need to tell you, he said, if your screams are anything to go by, which I thought was a bloody cheek myself. I mean, for all he knew, I could have stubbed me toe on the foot of the bed or damaged a ligament or something; don't laugh, these things happen. Well, I chucked him after that, well what would you do, I mean, bleeding Cornflakes for heaven's sake, and no milk neither. Shredded Wheat perhaps or even Coco Pops, but Cornflakes, for heaven's sake. Not that I'm averse to taking a little of your rough action when you can get it, when the moment arises, you know, you eye up a cute fellow and before you know it it's up against the toilet walls, a bit of spillage on the skirt, a quick wipe down with a Kleenex and it's back to Margery who's still in the queue ordering the drinks; you know, that kind of thing.

'Anyway. What did the accommodation officer say? *Sensible shoes, Patricia, whatever you do, wear a pair of sensible shoes, with all those hills*. For the life of me, I'm hopeless with regional accents, never mind Scottish. When I rang in, I had all the forms they sent me but I couldn't make head nor tail of them, I'm telling you. It was about a week after receiving the letter of acceptance. It took me two days to get back to earth, I were that bad from excitement, like. And you know how it is once you get talking, you get on to other things, like. God, I'm dreading me phone bill when it comes in.

'Yes, how long has it been? I've almost forgotten the

place. Apart from Margery and James. Talking about Cornflakes and sex, that reminds me. Clivewhatsisface, from a couple of years back. Yes, that Clive, ginger-headed Clive, I know, I couldn't believe it neither but hey, I'm getting all moist just thinking about it. Just before he popped his clogs. B&Q that Sunday, I'm telling you, if there weren't a crowd around, believe you me, I'd have joined in the queue with the rest of them. And it would've been a long one as well. Right up to the Welston Old Road. I wasn't the only one, believe you me. I saw the look on some of the faces. That bottle-blonde shop assistant who kept on mopping Clive's forehead with her hanky, those two old biddies cooing, *Are you all right dear, how about a cup of tea?*, indeed! That St John's Ambulance man hovering in the background waiting for an opportune moment to administer first aid. I wasn't fooled. Talk about butter wouldn't melt in their mouths, yeah right. I read about something similar in Northern Ireland, with the soldiers in the barracks and the local lasses. The *Sun* I think, or was it the *Guardian*; anyway, every night like clockwork, a bunch of the local girls would wait outside the barrack gates for the soldiers to come off duty and they'd have sex with the squaddies right there and then. The allure of danger I think the article said, a lethal cocktail of danger, sweat, khaki and boot polish – must've been the *Guardian*, you don't get words like lethal cocktail in the *Sun*, confuse the readers it would. Still, it's a sad business all around when you think about it. Poor Clivewhatsisface, if only he knew, eh, the effect he'd on us back then, he'd have been right made up. That Sunday afternoon at B&Q, with him holding that industrial-size hammer, laying into all them tiles and paint and kitchen units and sinks and the look in his eyes and the dust and the sweat pouring down his face and his damp ginger hair clinging to his face like clingfilm . . . *Rice Krispies!!*

The time, 2.45 pm, 26 April 1985; the place, a train somewhere in the middle of the Oxfordshire countryside, and the last thing on Margery's mind was 'Poor Clivewhatsisface.'

'Poor Clive, my foot. The stupid bastard's been asking for it. I wouldn't need to go behind his back if he wasn't such a right dickhead. Besides, what he doesn't know won't hurt him, and if he finds out, who cares? They're only WI numbers anyway. A pile of them in the old storeroom at the end of the first floor corridor. Trish was right.'

Even so, it was a nice enough train journey. Factories, rubbish tips, half-completed motorways, interspersed with brand-new Barratt-home estates. Not as scenic as the goings-on inside her head. This dream was more vivid, more surreal, and more besides, and was typical of the dreams Margery had been having lately.

Inside your head you could go anywhere. Hills and valleys rolling over the horizon, flocks of sheep for miles and miles – much better than talking to strangers sat next to you. But Margery wasn't in the mood for such peaceful spectacles right now. All she could think about was clinging on to the cliff edge by her fingernails. A gust of wind blew her skirt over her head, revealing Marks and Spencer's knickers with the labels cut off. She could hear her mother's advice right now.

'Wear a clean pair of knickers every day. You never know what might turn up.'

There was a jagged ledge just below her right foot. And as she tried to stretch for it her hand lost its grip. Not enough for her to fall but enough to make her swear out loud.

'Bloody Nora,' she said, which took her by surprise, as it had been years now since she'd said anything like that. Nowadays it was fucking hell or for fuck's sake, anything with fuck in it. The last time she could remember saying bloody Nora was back in school, the first year in Miss Simms' maths class. She got detention for it. Or that was how she liked to imagine it anyway, moments like this, hanging from a cliff's edge by her fingertips, rolling fields and sheep, lots of sheep.

The 10.45 train from Manchester Piccadilly to Oxford, change at Banbury, then on to Chippenham Wiltshire, a taxi from the station and in fifteen minutes it would be Holme Lodge, and a two day conference for senior managers and executives, though she knew the only reason she was there was because no one else knew a thing about microprocessors. Still, it was only a couple of days, and the company was paying so hey, what the hell. Besides, she wasn't short of ways to pass the time, especially on a four-and-a-half-hour train journey.

On these journeys inside your head you could picture all sorts. Hills, gorges, lots of sheep. Bare right foot stuck on a jagged ledge, shoe somewhere between Ramsbottom and Salford. And now to cap it all, a talking crag rock face like an old man that had seen it all. Still, for a talking crag rock face it seemed friendly enough. Friendly enough to talk to, open up her heart to, get things off her chest and all that. And why not, it wasn't like she was going anywhere.

'I'm not going too fast, am I? I mean, I'm not out of me depth, am I? Being here and all, on the train to Holme Lodge. Senior Information Technology Officer at the age of twenty-three. Unheard of for anyone at Samson Brothers, never mind a woman, a twenty-three-year-old woman at that and not even a steady boyfriend. Three steps away from an office in the executive suite, Paul Sinclair reckons. Three steps away from the executive suite. Three steps from heaven. Oh my giddy aunt.'

Hanging from a cliff's edge by her fingertips, rolling fields and sheep, lots of sheep, her skirt blown over her head and if she wasn't mistaken she wasn't wearing any knickers after all.

'It would be all right, wouldn't it, if I let go. It won't hurt much when I hit the rocks. You'd say wouldn't you, if it would hurt that is, you've got that kind of face? No, don't ask why, seems a good idea, that's all. If I just let me fingers slip just a little, it'd be over in a moment, wouldn't it? I wouldn't feel a thing, yes? Let me fingers go, like this, just a little, just like this . . .'

Margery opened her eyes. More fields than before as well as the Barratt homes, only now they were detached houses with bigger gardens, a Bentley or Mercedes in the drive, or both, not to mention the occasional covered-over swimming pool.

'I know all this is just an inferiority complex which left unchecked could very easily manifest itself into unthinking hostility, but I can't help it really – bloody southerners.'

fifteen

It had been on the cards for a long time now, the first set of voluntary redundancies. A year's salary tax free, offered to a selected number. One hundred employees or so, chosen on merit, age, and any other criteria the company saw fit. All of which was intended to soften the blow for the next round of redundancies, which would neither be voluntary, nor come with a year's salary tax free, and would amount to a reduction of the total workforce by fifty-five percent across the board over a period of two years, with several sections being phased out completely wherever the company saw fit. Not that the Management would admit to any of this, and anyone caught spreading such rumours would be dealt with accordingly.

All this had been on the cards for a long time now, and so it turned out on that fateful Thursday morning as each department was finally told the good news about the offer of a limited number of voluntary redundancies, across the board, one hundred and ten employees selected on merit, age, etc. And it went without saying there was no mention whatsoever of the proposed second wave. And as this was the Contracts Department it was left to Reg Prentice to give out the glad tidings, though it was hard to discern much cheer in the expression on his face. But with Reg, you knew his heart was in the right place at least. It couldn't be easy for him, giving out news like this, however positive. Still, Reg being Reg Prentice, it would be ages before he was done, so now was as good a time as any to talk amongst yourselves, discussing other more pressing matters in hand.

And as per usual it was one person doing the talking and everyone else doing the listening – in this case the talker was Jack Taggert, a Test Engineer at Samson Brothers for two years now, after ten years at Macdougalls McClain, trains and locomotive manufacturers, based at Holden Industrial Park before it went bust.

'As I was saying, the Aviation Authority had a device for testing the strength of windshields on aeroplanes. The device itself was a gun that launches a dead chicken at a plane's windshield at approximately the speed the plane flies, the theory being that if the windshield doesn't crack from the carcass impact, it'll survive a real collision with a bird during flight. Well, in principle anyway. As I was saying, we'd been developing a brand-new, speedy locomotive, the PPL3, and this seemed like the ideal opportunity to get our hands on the device. Mainly to test the windscreens, of course. Same theory as a plane flying if you think about it. So the company arranged a loan for a minimum of six months and the device was delivered, set up and everything, ready for testing. And on the first day of testing the chicken was loaded and fired. Well, where shall I start? The ballistic chicken shattered the windshield, went through the engineer's chair, broke an instrument panel and embedded itself in the back wall of the engine cab. Of course we were stunned. We hadn't planned for anything like that. We could have sworn we'd set up the equipment according to instructions. So we wrote back to the Aviation Authority asking them to recheck our test procedures to see if everything was done correctly. They wrote back to us with a five-page letter pretty much agreeing every step of the way, with only the one recommendation:

' "It's better if the chicken is not frozen." '

Nevertheless, as is usually the case with these things, there was always someone who saw the benefits. In fact, Matt was absolutely ecstatic. The prospect of voluntary redundancy with a year's salary was too good to be true. He had to pinch himself a couple of times to make sure he wasn't imagining it. Of course he knew that this was only a sweetener, and that there were more redundancies to follow, but hey, what the hell, he'd planned on leaving anyway to set up business full time. The confectionery stall on the market, the catering business, and if things went to plan, the old bike-repair shop on Tram Street. As neither of them knew the first thing about bikes, they'd planned on turning it into a newspaper corner shop. The original price had been £10,000 but the owner was prepared to accept £8,000. And with the prospect of the redundancy money, well, as far as Matt was concerned it was zippedidoodaa zippedeyay. He couldn't wait to tell Joan the good news tonight.

'Only after *Benny Hill*, of course. Steady on. First things first.'

Reg cleared his throat. He hated making announcements like this. Like it wasn't obvious to everyone what was really going on, but still, it was more than his job's worth to express his opinions willy nilly. He cleared his throat again, just to make sure. There was always some bugger who wouldn't quite hear what was being said, only instead of asking right away they'd leave it until about six months later, until all the papers had been signed and the ink had dried and then they'd come up to you and say, *Hey Reg, what about this, that and the other*, and when you told them it was too late and the applications should have been in weeks ago they would play mary hell and the next minute the unions would be up your arse.

Reg cleared his throat again. One couldn't be too careful.

'The actual sum offered would be dependent on the total years of service, age and present salary – exactly how much I couldn't say but in two weeks' time the actual figures will be announced and each employee will be sent a memo with said information. Meanwhile, if there's anyone has any other questions, my office is open all week and I can assure you that discretion will be the order of the day.'

Still, it was pretty obvious to everyone what was going on and Irene stood there, clutching her handkerchief like it was really hurting, trying hard to hold back the tears. The sudden memory of her mother dying two years ago came rushing back like it was yesterday. It wasn't like it wasn't expected at the time, the doctor said it could be anything between a couple of weeks, a couple of months and a couple of years. It turned out to be four months in the end. Nothing in particular really, the doctor said, just old age, which was understandable as she was getting pretty ancient, but still, with all the medicines and technology they have nowadays . . .

'You'd think there'd be some sort of treatment for it,' said Irene to the doctor at the time, just after he'd told her the bad news, advising her to bring the bed down into the living room perhaps, save the walking upstairs.

'I mean, it's 1983 for goodness sake. There was something on *Tomorrow's World* only last week about this very same thing, I'm sure there was,' said Irene, at the time, about two years ago, almost to the day in fact – a bit of a coincidence really, but wasn't that always the case when it came to bad news?

Henry tapped Irene on the shoulder.

'Are you okay, luv?'

'No I'm not, Henry, no I'm most certainly not.'

Henry looked at the clock. Quarter to twelve.

'Reg'll be done soon. You know Reg. I don't think he'll risk running into the lunch break. Even he's not *that* stupid.'

'Do you think so Henry?' said Irene.

'I'll put money on it, you'll see,' said Henry.

And afterwards, after much discussion and scratching

of heads in the canteen and the pub, it soon became clear that there had been similar meetings going on in each department, all of them at the same time. Almost the same words as well, like it was read from a script, which was pretty remarkable considering that no one saw Reg holding a sheet of paper.

'He must have been up all night rehearsing. Poor thing,' said Henry. 'Saying that, wait till Clive hears. It'll ruin his week.'

Which wasn't strictly true actually as Clive's week had been ruined for a long time now. And some hours later in a four-star hotel in the middle of the Oxfordshire countryside, Clive Barnes would be sat in a toilet cubicle, having suddenly left the meeting in the Arkwright Suite without a by your leave, just as Paul Sinclair was about to start a really interesting bit with the overhead projections and had already asked for the lights to be switched off. And now here was Clive, toilet seat down, talking to himself and not making a whole lot of sense neither.

'What the hell am I doing here? What the hell am I doing here, in this godforsaken place? The back of beyond in the middle of nowhere. On a Thursday as well. And look at the time, I must be mad. I'd like to say, *What the fuck am I doing here*, only I promised Maureen I'd cut down on the swearing. "It's not like you're on the shop floor," she said. Oh, what the hell, she isn't here. What the fuck fuck fuck am I doing here here here? There, that's much better. And while we're at it, is it me or is it hot in here?'

Still, the meeting in the Arkwright Suite went on regardless of anything back at Higher Maltby, not to mention the goings on inside Clive's head, which was a right dog's dinner in anyone's book.

'Paul Sinclair, him and his red braces, who the hell does he think he is? Been here all of five minutes and look at him. And he expects to come and lord it over us like he's cock of the north. He should stick to the management suite with the red carpet and posh lunches like the rest of the hoi polloi and leave the real world to those who can handle it. Saying that, it begs the question, doesn't it? Where's his time served, that's all I'll say? Where's his time served five-year apprenticeship, not to mention City and Guilds ONC HNC, day release and night school on the bus in the pouring rain, forget going to the pub afterwards because you're too shagged out? I mean, don't get me wrong, I'm all for your silver spoons Oxford Cambridge Henley Regatta, but if you come round here with your red braces and fake northern accent like he's one of us, well, you deserve all you get. Cock of the flipping north, king of the dung heap more like. If that's what he wants, he's welcome to it.'

Meanwhile, back at Higher Maltby, had anyone bothered to ask, then Reg would have had no problem admitting that as far as he was concerned, things had been going downhill for donkey's years now, ever since Samson Brothers decided to call a halt to the annual dinner dances at the Cranberry Hotel on the Oxford Road just across from the BBC studios in Manchester Piccadilly. Not that there was any such thing as the BBC back in the days when the first dinner dance took place. 1920, in fact. The then chairman of Samson Brothers decided in his infinite wisdom that the workers' morale needed boosting seeing as the war to end all wars had been over for a couple of years now and still productivity hadn't risen to what it had been before the fighting began.

'It's down on record, look it up if you don't believe me,' is what Reg Prentice would have said, had anyone bothered to ask – only they didn't, of course, especially now they were taking in the news about the redundancies.

Reg knew a great deal about local history, and any opportunity to talk about the subject he was in there like a flash.

'Marmite, Billy Cotton on the radio and the Tivoli bingo hall that used to be the old Gaumont cinema. Sixpence for a pint of mild, Jimmy Clitheroe, Ted Heath and his Orchestra, Old Mother Riley, the number fifty-two bus which ran every five minutes from Welston bus station, ten bob in them days would get you a week in Blackpool during the wakes, and for tuppence it was Reg Dixon playing the organ in the Tower Ballroom every afternoon, oh aye, the Costa del Sol, there was no need.'

Reg knew a lot about those things, the past and everything. When he retired he planned to write a book. But more immediate things first – the facts had to be explained in full and in no uncertain terms:

'Application dates, where to get the forms, redundancy packages, early retirements, possible relocation details, careers counselling, stuff like that. Pop into the office and we'll have a chat.'

The version of the song 'All That You Are' that most people were familiar with was the spoof version Peter Sellers sings as an old man in the bath. No one had a clue that the song itself was from a failed Broadway musical by Jerome Kern during the 1940s, the name of which no one could remember, which wasn't surprising as it was the last musical he ever wrote. But all that was neither here nor there because at that very moment, as Reg was giving out the news about the redundancies, every single one of them in the office: Irene, Matt, Henry, Phil, Mary, Karl, John Marks, David Scott, the two Roberts, Nick Monday, Jane Bucks, Claire from Accounts who just so happened to be using the photocopier as the one on the ground floor had broken down yet again; the lot of them, at that very moment in time, had that same song singing in their heads, as Reg was giving out the news about the redundancies. Even young Pete Price who was on a three-month secondment as part of the on-the-job industrial training for his second year of the ONC in Engineering, who must have been all of two years old when the Peter Sellers record was in the charts. All of which was pretty uncanny really – the odds of that happening, as some wag had said on the telly only the night before – more chance of eight score draws coming up on the pools, or being struck by lightning twice on the run. Pretty uncanny but somehow appropriate, because even though the Peter Sellers record was meant to be a spoof it was somehow just right for that moment; lush orchestral strings accompanied the lament of an old man who'd seen more than his fair share of life, whose only wish now was to enjoy simple pleasures such as soaking in a hot bath and singing at the top of his voice to the accompaniment of a full orchestra and having no one telling him to shut up. Even so, all good things must come to an end and slowly but surely the implications of Reg's words began to sink in.

'You know, Irene,' said Henry, 'I forget sometimes, what it is we do here. I mean, Samson Brothers PLC and all. What is it we *actually* do here? Yes, you're right, of course I know, but sometimes, Irene, I'm telling you, I'm at a loss sometimes.'

'Are you sure you're all right, Henry?' said Irene. 'I'll fetch a seat if you like, rest your legs.'

'You're a dear, Irene. You're a saint, you know that, don't you?'

Meanwhile, some hours later, two hundred miles down the motorway and a few A-roads, in the men's toilets of a four-star hotel in the middle of the Oxfordshire countryside, things had gone from bad to worse.

'I mean, it was horrible really, for a ten-year-old to know stuff like that, that the world's against the likes of him from the very start and if you're not in the right class right away you've got no bleeding chance. I'm talking about the eleven-plus, of course, what do you think I was talking about? Last year in the Juniors. All year we were being taught to pass the eleven-plus, practice tests every Monday, Wednesday and Friday after assembly, only it turned out we were being taught to fail. Because we did, all of us in 4B. We were 4B and only those in 4A were allowed to pass. You don't believe me, do you? Ask anyone in 4B if they passed then, go on, you ask them. Not even Carol James or Heather Bailey and they got As in all the practice tests, and they lived on the posh new housing estate round the corner from school. Go on, you ask them. We were 4B and we weren't allowed to pass and that was that. I'm telling you, it's a horrible thing for a ten-year-old to know. I cried when me mother opened the letter, I did, I cried. I'm telling you, it was horrible, really really horrible.'

And it was still some time later and it was still the middle of the Oxfordshire countryside, and it was still a four-star hotel and the cubicles of the men's toilets, and if Clive had been a horse he'd have been shot by now.

'I'm beggared if I know, I mean, one minute it's a Sunday morning and the wallpaper in the entrance is peeling off and Maureen says why not to pop over to B&Q for some grouting on the way back from buying the papers, and the next minute I'm in St Luke's Accident and Emergency having me head bandaged. Mind you, when I think about it, something had to crack, it had been on the cards for ages when I think back. You've been in B&Q haven't you, or one of those DIY stores sprouting up all over the place – like wild fire they are, one minute there's an open field the size of a football pitch, two months later there's a whole new shopping centre with parking, pizza bar, a burger shop and not enough toilets and . . . I'm going off the point aren't I? Well, that's how it gets me with these places, I just want to spit. Don't get me wrong. I was like the next guy, all that DIY stuff under one roof, like a sweet shop for grown-ups.'

And not only was it still the middle of the Oxfordshire countryside and a four-star hotel and not only had the horse been shot, but the carcass had been chopped up, boiled down as glue, poured into half-pint jars and shipped off to ironmongers and stationery shops across the country.

'I suppose it all kicked off about a year back when Maureen says she would quite like one of those conservatories like the one in the brochure, only with the price quoted by those three contractors you'd need a second mortgage at least. So after a little adding up, you decide in a moment of madness to build one yourself, despite Maureen's protestations. And you reassure her that you've worked everything out in the minutest detail, you even show her the lists you've made out on five sides of A4 sheets, outlining each stage with times and appropriate costs, with the final figure for savings made underlined in the right-hand bottom corner so that even Maureen couldn't miss it. But was she impressed?

' "Why don't I just phone the bank, see if I could arrange a loan," she said. "Interest rates aren't bad at the moment, I read it in the newspapers."

'None of which goes anywhere near to explaining why I took that hammer to all that stuff back then, does it? I don't fully understand meself neither but there you go, just one of those things really. Happens to the best of us. I don't remember much after that if I'm honest, only

Maureen coming to see me at the hospital afterwards. I'm not kidding neither. I know it sounds convenient, me losing me memory and all afterwards, but honest, that's how it was. I haven't a clue how that hammer got into my hand like that in the first place. Five thousand pounds' damage all told they reckoned it was. Not that I had to pay a penny, the powers that be came to the conclusion that the publicity would do more harm than good. Which was just as well really seeing as I spent over two thousand pounds two months back. The conservatory of course, what do you think I've been talking about for the last hour, for goodness sake? Still, it's a funny old world, isn't it? Patios, conservatories, they pale into insignificance don't they, you know, compared to other matters? Not that Maureen ever said I told you so, though she would've been well within her rights to do so. Oh and yes, you guessed, it hasn't been built. Well, with one thing and the other, it hardly matters now, does it?'

sixteen

Henry's Makeup Tips 4 Lips by Henry Johnson

... Saying that, I'm a great fan of kippers meself for Sunday morning breakfast, grilled with a poached egg, mushrooms and buttered toast with lots of butter. And if the weather's fine I'm in the garden all day. Pottering about, whatever needs doing, there's always something. Still, the neighbours' tree is a right nuisance, or at least it was until the man from the council said I was in me rights to cut down any branches which extended over into my garden. I'd only rung in to enquire about emptying the bins for next Monday on account of it being a Bank Holiday, and you know how it is, you get talking like and you end up saying all sorts; he tells me about his son's glue-sniffing addiction and I end up telling him about the neighbours' leylandii and how it was blocking out the light from the vegetable patch and how it had right upset me like, so much so that we'd even considered moving house. And he said don't do that as that was totally unnecessary and then he went on to explain that under some bylaw I was perfectly within my rights to lop off the offending branches. And so I did, two weeks ago, and he's not said nothing so far, Don, the neighbour. Still, as the wife's always saying, you can't trust no one who has venetian blinds as well as net curtains on their front room window. It's his wife, Mildred, I feel sorry for. With her not working and all. Not for over twenty years now.

Did I say she used to be a policewoman? Who? Mildred, of course. Don's missus, that's how they met apparently. He was a carpenter doing repairs at the station and, well, one thing led to another – his words not mine – and it's been over twenty years now. She was only a young policewoman at the time but you know how it is when you're in the wrong place at the wrong time.

. . . Oh dear, I'm doing it again, aren't I? Okay then. Oh yes, lips. I like to leave the lips to the last as a special treat. I usually wait until I get my clothes on so I don't get lipstick on anything.

Select the right colours. Choose a lipstick and matching liner – ideally the liner should be just very slightly darker, though the same colour will do. The purpose of the liner is not to outline the lips but to create a defined lip. Lipstick by itself tends to bleed and not go on in a straight line. Your lipstick and liner should also complement the blush you use. Sometimes I use the lipstick colour as blush. I save lipstick for the last step after everything else is on –

hair, clothes, nails, etc. This way you can make certain that the lipstick colour you select works. If you're not sure and have a variety, experiment. I have several different-coloured wigs, ranging from brunette to brown to red to blonde. Talking of wigs . . .

Apparently she would dye her hair to get it blonde like that. You know, those two, who murdered them kiddies on the moors. Well the woman anyway, not the bloke. He were into bikes and Nazi memorabilia amongst other things. Shame he didn't leave it there, eh? Would have saved everyone a lot of fuss and bother. Like I said, she had more of a mousy brown in real life that one. They had to send in for hair bleach during the court appearances. That was one of Mildred's duties, being the only police-woman on duty and all. Hair bleach, biros and writing pad to take shorthand as well as a fresh packet of Murray Mints every day. There was a corner shop across the road from the crown courts so it wasn't too much bother. Which is more than I can say for the rest of this section on lips. I wish I hadn't started the damn thing now. More bother than it's worth if you ask me. Oh well, soonest done soonest mended. You won't mind if I speed things up a little, no of course you don't.

Line your lip and smile really wide, like this see, as wide as you can to stretch your lip out, then line the outer edge of your lips all the way around, the goal is to get a straight line – a q-tip will erase mistakes quickly and easily. Then take a lipstick brush and spread it around, blending it into the lip line you've already created, after which press your lips together and then blot with a tissue, like this see, to tone the colour down a tad, unless it's a dramatic look you're after (starlet/fifties/slut, etc.); sometimes I'll take powder and cover my lips very lightly as this gives a softer look. What comes next, oh yes, one last bit, if you have large lips you can make them smaller by liplining within your lip and covering the outer portions with foundation. There, that's that out of the way. Right, now where was I up to? Oh yes, those tapes.

Anyway, it was the court case and all and the evidence was being read out, well, it came to the tapes didn't it, those tapes, you know, those tapes, you must know what I'm talking about, anyway, it was like the judge said at the time – I wasn't there of course, I only heard later from Don because Mildred told him – anyway, the judge said that in his opinion we have no right to exclude the public but anyone who wishes not to listen should leave now. Only what was she supposed to do, I mean, she was there on duty wasn't she? She couldn't have left the court even if she wanted to. Still, it was like Don said, it's only afterwards you realise the damage's been done. They call it post-traumatic syndrome, there's a name for everything nowadays. Don't know if that's a good thing or bad meself, there's probably a posh name for nappy rash I bet you, still, that's what the doctor called it and in her case, well, you could hardly argue, could you? I mean, the evidence is right there in front of you. I mean, we've been neighbours for ages now and I can count on one hand how many times she's been outside, even for barbecues. Stays in and plays the piano all day, and pretty good by the sound of it, well, who wouldn't be with all that practice?

A good dancer in her time as well, Don says, a mean twister in her day, won medals for it. It's the same with all of us, isn't it? If it's not one thing it's the other, we're all just that much from losing it, don't you think? Don't believe if you don't want, but believe you me, most of us, we're that much from the screaming abdabs. Take me for example . . .

seventeen

The story about the boy playing football in the streets was Maureen's favourite, closely followed by the one about the lollipop man being run over by a lorry in front of all the kids in the infants school playground, whilst Clive and his mates looked on, clinging to the schoolyard gates, straining themselves to the top in order to get a better view. Never mind that the lollipop man's head was bleeding all over the place. Which was pretty sick in anybody else's book, but not for a bunch of schoolkids having their dinnertime break. According to the piece, it was more fun than playing football or watching *Batman* on the telly or eating fish and chips from the newspaper, which just about sums it up really.

It was Wilma's idea to send all the stories and poems to a publisher. Maureen hadn't even heard of the word Anthology before. But then Wilma had always been a bit of reader, having passed her English Literature O level, and now after not seeing each other for so many years, it was like she had never been away. A shame about the circumstances that brought them together again after all these years, but as they say, one door shuts and another one opens.

And as for book readings and public speaking, it was like most things really. With preparation, practice and a glass of water handy, it wasn't such an ordeal after a couple of times. Still, according to the publishers, it'd all be over in a couple of weeks' time, which was just as well. These last two months had been so hectic with newspapers, radio and even north-west telly, one of those local early news reports, not to mention being a panel member on a Q/A session for local writers at the 16th Annual Glossop and Tintwistle Arts Festival. Not that anyone minded in the least that she wasn't actually the writer. They still came in their droves, so much so that for five weeks now the book had been on the top ten list of best-sellers at Sherbridge and Huttons bookshop in Welston shopping precinct next to Burton's Menswear.

It was like Wilma had said all along, *Think Jim Reeves, Buddy Holly, James Dean. Folk are daft like that. They can't get enough of you when you're dead.*

The first piece was about walking carefully along the pavement, taking extra special care not to step on any crack as that would mean instant vaporisation like being zapped by a laser gun; then came a twelve-line love poem that made you want to cry every time you read it; next a thousand-word piece looking yearningly back to the 1970 World Cup which Brazil won with Pelé and Jairzinho, full of nostalgia for those innocent days of black and white television, Billy Smart's Circus, Georgie Best and Bobby Charlton, listening to Radio Luxembourg under your bedsheets, *Top of the Pops* when it was held in an old church on Dickinson Road, and you could buy three ice cornets with two chocolate flakes, nuts and hundreds and thousands and still have enough change from a thrupenny bit for a *Beano*. The piece ended with the line – 'I want my childhood back' – which never failed to bring a smile and a sigh from the audience, each member transported back to days gone by. Sixteen years of marriage to a guy and then suddenly, out of the blue, a cupboard drawer in the garage full of short stories and poems. Thank heaven she hadn't stuck to her plan to throw out all the stuff from the garage without first having a sort-out.

There were twenty pieces altogether, six poems, twelve short stories and two pieces that could have been articles in the newspaper. It had been one hell of an effort even to piece them together from the paper and junk they were lying amongst. Initially, Wilma had put together the most complete three pieces and sent them off to her friend who worked in a publishers in Hebden Bridge. And when her friend at the publishers had written back saying *wow*, there might be something here, only then were the remaining sheets sorted out and the twenty or so best pieces assembled. The rest were placed in a plastic bag labelled IMPORTANT – DO NOT THROW AWAY, at the advice of Wilma's friend the editor.

Poor Clive. If he'd known how much fuss all his scribbles had caused he'd have been right made up.

Still, it was all for the best in the long run, him not being around, because she quite enjoyed the attention, if truth be known, especially the book readings. In fact, a female voice was just perfect for reading stories about the adventures of a little boy. And with all that enthusiasm and the occasional squeak or giggle from Maureen, if the listener closed their eyes then to all intents and purposes, they were listening to a ten-year-old boy growing up in back-to-back terraced houses in the late 1950s, early 1960s, when Harold Macmillan said we'd never had it so good. And after each reading there would be a question and answers session where the audience were free to ask about the book and about Clive and what kind of a man he must have been to write such moving stories. And Maureen would always answer truthfully, and admit that she hadn't a clue that Clive had written so much. She knew he'd started writing about four years back and when he'd showed her his first efforts she had thought they were a load of rubbish – *not that I told him so exactly, I didn't fancy the sulks* – so she was just as surprised as they were if truth be known. And when they asked her why she thought he could write such wonderful prose, she would shrug her shoulders and then go on to describe the kind of man that Clive was. Nothing too personal, of course, just things like how he would scratch his balls when he thought no one was looking, his perpetual habit of making lists, how he had to have his chips just right, a couple of extra minutes in the chip pan until they were almost burnt. And of course it went without saying about the snoring. And how on Christmas morning he would make her breakfast in bed and they'd sit there in bed watching the cartoons and the nativity service. And the audience would laugh along with her, as it was pretty clear that Clive was just a regular person, no better or worse than the next guy really, and the wives would nod in recognition and then turn to their husbands as if to say, yes, but why can't you do anything so special?

And it would invariably be like this, the Q/A session, a cosy little affair like a chat in the living room with friends and cups of tea, all it needed was net curtains closed and the gas fire turned up and the telly switched off and it would have been home from home. And it went without saying they were on to a winner because the crowds and the responses were the same every night, whether it was the local library or the big book shop in Deansgate. And with each one it became easier and more cosy, almost as if she had really needed it, needed to unload herself, to talk about things amongst friends. Read the stories, sign books, talk afterwards, pass round the tea and biscuits – fig rolls, anyone? Not that the publishers had any complaints. According to their last letter, a second print run was in hand, and after that, a new collection, fingers crossed, pieced together from all the papers left in the plastic bag labelled IMPORTANT – DO NOT THROW AWAY.

Maureen had been thinking of having a baby for several months so when Wilma brought up the subject that Sunday afternoon she almost jumped at the chance. She'd been doing some reading at the library on the subject. It was amazing what you could find if you asked the right questions – the librarians were always more than willing to help. After which she paid a visit to Dr Wright, her GP for fifteen years, who was very sympathetic of hers and Wilma's situation, and gave her a complete run down of all possible medical options, and implications legally, financially and morally. Maureen even took the liberty of approaching someone from work who she'd had an inkling would be more than willing to assist with no questions asked. And she was right too because when she asked him during dinner break with no one within earshot, explaining exactly what was expected from him and how to go about it with the least amount of fuss and bother, and what was expected from him after the event, if everything went to plan, fingers crossed, he was so pleased to have been asked that he broke down in tears.

So when Wilma brought the subject up out of the blue that Sunday afternoon, two years ago to the day almost since Clive's B&Q episode, Maureen was so well prepared that Wilma had to repeat the question just to make sure that Maureen had fully understood her. Conceiving a baby was a serious business all round, even more so in their situation, and all the options and implications had to be thought out thoroughly. But Maureen just laughed and asked Wilma to pass the remote control as there was no way she was watching *Songs of Praise*, there had to be something else on the other side.

'If not, pop over to the video shop will you, love? Anything you like so long as there's no violence. Yeah, *Kramer versus Kramer*, that'll be nice. The dinner will be done when you get back. And on the way, pop into the off-licence for a Blue Nun. One from the fridge okay, there won't be enough time to chill it before dinner. I'll explain everything afterwards, okay? Don't look so worried, chuck, I heard you the first time, I'm not deaf.'

eighteen

A strike, a picket line, lousy weather, students from the local tech carrying SWP banners and handing out leaflets, and twenty or so men, mostly from the shop floor, a few from the offices, with only a brazier burning coal to keep them warm, spouting the usual nonsense with each other as they did at work or in the sauna or the pub or at football matches, only now they were outside in the freezing cold – pretty standard really for a strike.

As stories went, the one about the man shouting *Taxi Taxi*, after being abandoned in the middle of the Atlantic Ocean during World War II, was one of the better ones bandied about to boost morale that morning. Fred Brown's Uncle Ernie had been a sailor on board a merchant ship crossing the Atlantic with a cargo load of bananas when it was torpedoed by a German U-boat which just so happened to be passing at the time. Or else it would have been if Fred hadn't gone to the toilet and Sam Buttress, one of the fitters from Metalclad and

Plastering, saw the chance to get matters off his chest.

'Them taxis, ages coming they are, I'm telling you,' said Sam. 'Waiting bloody hours for one in Welston centre after closing time, might just as well have walked it. Rang the wife in the end. Thursdays is her evening class. Calligraphy, that where they do all that posh handwriting. Waste of time I tell her but you can't say nothing nowadays, even when you're married to 'em. Ended up sleeping on the couch. Mind you, she's not been the same since our Trixy died. Our Trixy, the dog, silly, Jack Russell. Been over a year now since our Trixy committed suicide. Of course it was suicide. Why else would it throw itself off the balcony? Hey up, Ron's here with the butties.'

Ron was Ron the union man, who twenty minutes before had been around taking orders for sandwiches and drinks. Compliments of the union, which was only to be expected during strikes – it helped that his sister-in-law ran the buttie bar on the corner of North Street just down the road. Once the sandwiches and drinks had been handed round and Fred Brown had done his business in the toilet it was business as usual.

'Every Christmas for as long as I can remember,' said Fred. 'Me mam and her stories about Uncle Ernie. Him in middle of the Atlantic Ocean shouting *Taxi Taxi*. Like that film *The Cruel Sea* with Jack Hawkins wearing a duffle coat. Every bleeding Christmas. Even as a kid I'd had it up to here. Mam said it was typical of Uncle Ernie. He had a right sense of humour. Anyone else would've kept their mouth shut and drowned in peace but oh no, not our Ernie. No, he didn't leave a will, me Uncle Ernie. Like it matters in the end. End up as fish food anyway. It's all the same to the fishes, will or no will, eh? To be or not to be, like. *Tuxi Tuxi*. No, me Uncle Ernie wasn't into Shakespeare. He was a bit of a comedian, that's all, Mam said.'

And as picket lines went it was the usual stuff – two groups of men, about twenty in each, one group outside the factory gates and the other by the office entrance as that was the minimum number that constituted an official picket line. Fewer than that and the picket would be illegal. And sure enough, there was a policeman on hand to enforce that law if necessary. Not that there was much need for it, but any opportunity for extra overtime was nothing to sneeze at. It wasn't like it was the miners, anyway, and even if it was, two of his credit cards were up to the limit and the bank was threatening to make him pay up his overdraft of £750 immediately, which was a shame as he and his girlfriend both had their hearts set on a spring break to the States. Still, it was none of his business what they were striking about, or why the whole thing kicked off in the first place. It had all begun that Thursday afternoon back in April, the day the workforce had been told the news about the voluntary redundancies. Not that this was the reason they were out on strike, though it would have been quite understandable. And nor did it have anything to do with the gun siege that had begun about two o'clock at number 10 Acomb Street that same afternoon, which was why everyone had been out in the car park, and which ended up with one man being shot dead and a four-page spread in the *Manchester*

Evening News as well as a late-night debate on the TV on the alarming escalation in gun-related crime.

And if truth be known, no one could say exactly what triggered off the strike in the first place, those being the days when any excuse was taken to go out on strike, however slight (for example, the boilermakers at Smiths Hydraulics and Electrometers had only just returned to work last week after a three-month dispute on account of their management refusing them permission to finish work ten minutes early on Christmas Eve), but go out on strike they most certainly did. Top of most people's list of grievances would have been Simon Standage, for issuing ultimatums to everyone outside in the car park to hurry up and get a move on, with the threat that those caught loitering would be sacked on the spot, immediately – asking for trouble in anyone's book. A close second might have been the announcement of voluntary redundancies that same morning, as and where the company saw fit. Which anyone with an ounce of sense knew would not be the end of it, not by a long chalk. Or maybe it was just the fact that it was a hot, sunny day and everyone was having so much fun out there doing their own business, whatever took their fancy, and it had been such a long time since anyone had had as much fun as this – not since the war for some, it was that far back – and it would have been a real shame to end it all by having to go back in to work.

But strike they most certainly did. The start of the strike had been four weeks ago and now today, if anyone had had a mind to ask the pickets why they'd gone out on strike in the first place, they would have been hard pushed to give an answer. Which was always the case with these things but still, it was a lousy day even for May, though not as bad as the previous two days when it had chucked it down so hard that tents had to be put up for shelter. And as usual it was one person who did all the talking, not that anyone was complaining. So long as he kept to matters mundane.

'I'd just had a swim at the baths round the corner – earlybird swim, six-thirty to eight-thirty, thirty-two lengths every morning, equivalent to half a mile, and that's me set for the day – like I said, I'm on my way to work and I'm waiting for the bus. Anyway, there's a long queue at the bus stop because one hadn't come for ages and you know how it is with the buses, three turn up at once, but like I said there's a long queue so while those at the front get on the first bus I decide to go for the second one, especially as it had let off a lot of passengers, a bit cheeky like, but nothing out of the ordinary, everyone does it. Yes, its exactly like queuing by the tills in the supermarket and a cashier opens up a fresh till and those at the back of the queue rush to the newly open till, just like that. Perhaps it's not that cheeky after all, that's what I thought. But not the driver, oh no, he was right pissed off, I could see his face as I was getting on, but I thought sod it, I had me bus pass in me hand ready to flash it at him as I went past. But he was having none of it, the daft sod, and before I could take a seat he'd grabbed me by the throat and was threatening blue murder.

' "I said get off this fucking bus," he kept shouting, yes he did, gospel, in between the punches and shaking me about like a rag doll left, right and centre. It took all me effort just to stay on me feet and the bus I can tell you, what with me artificial leg and all – of course I didn't tell him I had an artificial leg, he never gave me a chance, punching and swearing like that. He found out in court, mind you, oh yes, took him to court all right. Charged with ABH, actual bodily harm, magistrates court, the one in the centre of town, car parking round there is pretty lousy even with me disability sticker. Of course he got the sack. Saying that, the reporter was right disappointed when he found out it wasn't cancer. How I lost me leg in the first place, didn't I say? I said it was a cyst only it kept on eating away at all me leg muscle and all but he wouldn't have it. It was in all the papers, you must have seen it, didn't I say, could've sworn I did? Anyway, you know now. Still, that reporter, he were right disappointed like, when I told him it wasn't cancer. He kept on saying, *Are you sure it wasn't cancer?* I had to put me foot down in the end or else he would have put down cancer all right. The *Evening News*. I went there right away, after going to the police and the hospital to have me tetanus jab. Apparently it's compulsory to have one of those tetanus jabs after an attack like that. Me, oh, scratches down the neck, a torn shirt, but that were it really. Yes, for a minute back there I thought I had a black eye, I thought I felt the swelling and all, you bet I was disappointed, you can't argue with a black eye in court. Saying that, the compensation came in handy and all. We'd our eyes on a new conservatory for a long time. Still, for someone who's blind, that Gerald didn't half give the bus driver what for.

I'm telling you, if I hadn't pulled him off he would've beat the living daylights out of him. That blind passenger with the white stick, I told you, of course I did, you mustn't have been listening. Anyway, this blind bloke, Gerald Stamp he was called I found out afterwards. Plays keyboards for this five-piece jazz funk group, Saints Alive, they do a weekly Friday session at the Opera Arms on Broad Lane, free if you're in by nine-thirty. Anyway this Gerald Stamp, he had the bus driver pinned up against the wall threatening blue murder, and if I hadn't jumped in the guy would've ended up in casualty. The bus driver, not Gerald, oh no, I'm telling you, never cross swords with a blind guy with a walking stick who plays keyboards for a jazz funk group. You must have seen it in the papers. Yes, I know I wasn't working here at the time but still, you couldn't miss it, it was all over the papers. Anyway, with all the punching and shaking and trying to stay on me feet and all you'd think I'd have been scared, yes, I'd have thought sc too, but the strangest thing, I'm telling you, the only thing I could think of at the time, in between all the punching and shaking and smashed windscreens – oh yes, I forget to mention that he threw me against the windscreen – anyway, it was the strangest thing but all I could think of was, *wow*, this would make a great story.'

Even so, all this was light relief compared to events about four weeks back, when the whole palaver kicked off. That Thursday afternoon, about a quarter past one, the fire alarm went and the whole office block had to be evacuated, on account of the gun siege across the road at number 10 Acomb Street.

There were set procedures to follow when evacuating the building – in case of fire, bomb scare, or other such emergencies – which had first been formulated during the war when effective evacuation meant saved lives – back in the days when the annual dinner dance at the Cranberry Hotel in Manchester Piccadilly was still the most eagerly anticipated evening of the working calendar. And following the dinner, speeches and wine toasting, the whole of the dining hall would join in a rousing rendition of everyone's favourite 'Down Middletown Way'. But all that was in the past – the dinner dances had stopped in 1969. And as far as Ted Janis the Safety Officer was concerned, if the twice-monthly fire alarm practice drills all ran as smoothly as this one, then there'd be no need for the twice-monthly practices in the first place. But then again he'd be out of a job, so why argue the toss when it was a cheese and pickle barm cake you wanted in the first place. As for everyone else, why look a gift horse in the mouth? Any excuse not to work, and if all it meant was standing in the car park then it was cheap at the price. With a bit of luck they'd be out there for a long time coming. Long enough to find something really interesting to take up the time – especially if the rumours were true about Acomb Street.

And after about five minutes there was so much going on in the car park that even if anyone had said anything about the gun siege at number 10 Acomb Street, and Darren Molloy Pearson holding his wife and son Darren Junior hostage with an AK Kalashnikov automatic he'd bought down the pub, they wouldn't have taken the slightest bit of notice anyway.

Latin American dance classes run by Marcus and Andrea Thompson. Second runners-up in the 1963 Lower Broughton ballroom competition, Salsa section, the medals were still on the mantelpiece after all these years. Not to mention three poker games, a bridge class, two pub quizzes and a debating session on 'The Chip Pan – the greatest invention since the wheel?' And if that wasn't enough, almost all of the cars had their boots open, selling everything from Mills and Boon paperbacks, second-hand Tupperware, home-made cakes and scones, Ann Summers exotic lingerie and sex-toys, car batteries, X-rated video tapes, tarot card predictions, homeopathic medicines and acupuncture sessions – £2.50 per hour including instructions on breathing and meditation. Mavis McCormick and her makeshift hairdresser's set up by the medical centre unit next to the main office – the nearest place to a hot water tap and electric sockets, and if it started to rain there was always the unit itself for shelter. Never mind that Ken Masters, one of the clerks in the Wages Department, or Daffodil Morrissey to his friends, wanted to use one of the electric sockets for his guitar amplifier. As far as Daffodil Morrissey was concerned, a ready-made crowd like this was too much of a godsend, a ready-made crowd to listen to his oft-practised rendition of Johnny Marr's guitar riff from the classic 'What Time is Now?' by The Smiths. None of which was cutting any ice with Mavis.

'I'd help out if I could,' said Mavis, 'but I've a two-thirty blue rinse in five minutes, Phil Smart is down for a full perm at three and there's at least five on standby in case of cancellations. You're not looking at anything being free before four-thirty at least.'

And there by the security guard's office, Dot Brindley from Purchases had set up a deck chair and large umbrella and was offering astrology, palm reading and tarot card predictions, £1.50 for fifteen minutes which was double the usual rate – all to be expected really, market forces being what they were.

Amongst all this was Matt, who had set up a small booth the size of a telephone box and was offering budget flights to the Canaries, Costa del Sol, Majorca, Benidorm, Ibiza, anywhere that was sunny really, and near Spain.

'We've had the idea for a long time now. Cut out the middle man, there's a packet to be made, I'm telling you.'

It wasn't long before the car park became so chocker with shoppers and lookers on that after a while the buses from the Welston Old Road had to be diverted to make an extra stop outside the factory gates to cope with the influx of passengers. And in case of further congestion, the local radio stations had traffic bulletins every fifteen minutes given by two helicopters flying overhead advising drivers on possible alternative routes.

Even so, the camera crews from the Granada Studios on Quay Street had no problems getting through, and in no time at all they'd set up shop and were in the process of interviewing Irene and her ex-husband Ralph. None of which had been the crew's intention when they had left the studios that afternoon. Originally they'd been sent as back-up to the crew doing the main report on the gun siege at number 10 Acomb Street. If Irene had had any idea that morning that she'd be doing an interview for the telly then she would have put on a new dress, or at least a new pair of high heels. But that was always the case, she was always being caught out, just like the sudden reunion with her ex-husband Ralph who she hadn't seen in six years, who just happened to be passing on his way to the bookies when he noticed all the commotion and thought he'd pop over for a look.

And if anyone had asked either of them why they had split up in the first place they'd have been hard pushed to give an answer, but still, this wasn't *Any Questions*, and feel-good pieces on the late-night slot were always good for ratings, especially with all the palaver going on across the road at Acomb Street. Like every other marriage, they'd set out with all the best intentions. A simple enough wedding really, St Luke's Church off the Welston Road, followed by a fish and chip supper back at Ralph's mam and dad's house afterwards. And after that it should have been straightforward really. Three kids, boys or girls, it didn't matter which, a terraced house round the corner from both the in-laws, bingo and the bookies on the same road round the corner. Still, the best laid plans . . .

'. . . of mice and men, eh?' said Irene.

'Of mice and men? A bit posh that for you, our Irene,' said Ralph.

'There's a million where that one came from, if you've got the time.'

'I hear there's a dinner dance at the Cranberry Hotel tonight,' said Ralph. 'Dinner dance, you know, over-fifties like, couples only. Yeah, that Cranberry Hotel, Manchester Piccadilly. Be like old times.'

If anyone had asked George whether he minded not being on the telly, then George would have said with all honesty that he wasn't bothered in the slightest, even though there might well have been a reason to interview him, seeing as it was almost twenty years ago to the day that the police found the body of his best mate, all curled and strapped up in a brown canvas sack in the airing cupboard like it was Christmas; in the airing cupboard of the house of that couple who killed all them kiddies on the moors. *Folk round 'ere still don't like to talk about it much.* No, George was quite relieved actually. And besides, he had quite enough to keep him occupied – a line of over twenty-five people waiting outside his kiosk decked out with a curtain like a confessional, wanting to talk to him. This was another of Matt's ideas – an old portaloo left over from when the extension to the office block was built, set up as a portable confessional. Only it was George who was doing most of the talking, which was understandable enough. It wasn't every day that your best mate was found dead in a canvas bag in an airing cupboard, however long ago. Still, even Matt had to admit it would have been a bit much to charge them fifty pence and all.

'Make it twenty-five pence,' said Matt, 'and if business drops off, knock sommat off. Not too much mind you, you still owe me ten weeks' pool money.'

Not that George had any complaints. A chance like this

might never come up again. So he was making the most of it and then some.

'Still, I've no complaint, I suppose. Okay, so he was me best mate and all but when compared to others, I mean, take round here for example. Those streets of terraced houses across the road from the office gates. Acomb Street, Peter Road, Alexandra Street and a couple of the others if me memory serves me right. Page fifty-six of the A to Z. Co-ordinates 5E to be exact, I looked it up the same afternoon Reg Prentice told me about it. I'm telling you, it's mind blowing, that's all I can say, mind blowing. Whole streets of men, decimated like that, all the men that were able to fight that is, with it being in the First World War. There's a big brass plaque on the factory gates with all their names embossed in gold-plated italics in alphabetical order, Reg said. Battle of the Somme or one of those battles, you couldn't tell one from the other, Reg said, up to their eyes in mud and corpses. He's read about all that stuff in the library, has Reg. To do with some research he's doing. He says he's writing a book. I mean, whole streets of men. Imagine it, eh? No of course you can't and why should you, eh? It's beyond imagination, that's what it is, just beyond imagination. And thank goodness as well, don't you think, I mean there are just some things that are, well, how can I put it, there are just some things that are best left only to the imagination.'

Meanwhile, Henry was at home, having sneaked away just after the fire alarm went off. A chance for an early start seeing as it was a Thursday, too good an opportunity to miss. Which was a pity for the spare camera crew because although reunion pieces were perfect for the late-night feel-good slots, when push came to shove, a cross-dressing engineer at a north-west engineering company would leave most pieces standing, hands down, and then some. But could you imagine Henry agreeing to being interviewed on the telly? Still, that camera crew didn't know what it was missing:

'Take you lot for example. You probably thought you'd be doing one of those feel-good pieces for the late-night slots, not worth getting out of bed for, I hear you say. Well there you go, just goes to show, doesn't it, don't count your chickens and all that. But who'd have thought, eh? Makeup tips from a cross-dressing engineer whose main philosophy in life is based on obscure mathematical formulae expressing the relationship between electromotive forces, electric currents and the resistance in a circuit, developed by a German physics professor at the University of Munich in 1827. And to what am I referring? It's funny you should ask.'

Not that this was any concern of the main camera crew. They were here to do a job, and one job only. And as long as the batteries were fully charged and no kids or dogs about to cause a nuisance then fingers crossed, it would all be done by tea-time, bar the shouting.

And back in the office building, in the lift in fact, if anyone had bothered to check, Ron Wild was fast asleep, which wasn't surprising what with all the shouting and screaming he'd been up to but still, it had been a fantasy of his for a long time now. Being stuck in a confined space, helpless and trapped, unable to escape. Buried alive in a coffin, locked in a small toilet, the smaller the better – so long as there was enough air to breathe. Why he hadn't thought of the lift before, God only knew. It was ideal really, a minute's walk from the shop floor. It was only pure luck that he'd been in the lift in the first place. Usually he sent his sick note by the internal mail box, but today he'd wanted to have a word with the Personnel Officer, face to face, to ask whether or not the rumours were true and if so, whether they would consider voluntary redundancy on medical grounds, on account of him being off sick so regularly. Bad back, high blood pressure, angina, swollen ankles – you name it, he'd had it, and he had doctors' notes if proof were needed. Still, an ill wind never blows as they say, and here he was, exhausted but satisfied from all that screaming and shouting, the helplessness of it all, which was exactly the point of the exercise. Being Faye Wray kidnapped by King Kong on top of the Empire State Building – *oh my!*

Meanwhile, some hours later, back in the men's toilets on the first floor at Holme Lodge, Clive Barnes couldn't give a monkey's one way or the other. He'd been past caring for a long while now. It was all much of a muchness really, a four-star hotel in the middle of the Oxfordshire countryside, Margery Watkins' sensible blouse and skirt producing quite the opposite effect to the one she'd intended. At the end of the day it was all about appearances really. Images, façades, fronts, which all amount to much the same thing. The bigger the brighter the better. Cardboard, papier mâché, candy floss, who cared? So long as the look was right then mission accomplished. TV companies worth millions on the stock market saved from bankruptcy by an overactive glove puppet by the name of Roland, female news presenters sent internal memos instructing them to show a bit more thigh, a B-movie actor leading the Western world, white shirt and bright red braces with colour slides and a scale model wheeled in on a trolley on cue – all of which amounted to much the same thing really. More work less pay.

Still, the new B&Q on the Snide Estate was real enough. The new B&Q on the Snide Estate off the Welston Old Road: row upon row, endless stacks of items for the home or garden. Bricks, tiles, skirting boards of various lengths, self-tapping screws, ceramic sink basins without the taps, stainless steel chairs stacked up to the ceiling, three-litre pots of grouting paste in all different colours – you name it, they had it. So long as it was for the house or the garden. And on top of that, whole kitchen suites, whole bedroom suites, whole bathroom suites in avocado so realistic you could turn on one of the taps and expect to get hot water. And over in the far corner near one of the rear exits to the car park, a working machine shop was set up, with band-saws, sanders, milling machines and industrial-size drills, screw-weighing machines just right for a bag of assorted nuts, so much so that the only thing missing was the clocking-on machine by the door.

'You know, back then when I said I couldn't remember a thing that went on. Bollocks, I remember everything. Every damn bleeding moment of it and I'm telling you it felt great, really great. You know how it is when everything suddenly comes together and it all makes sense. No you probably don't, do you? I guess not, only happens once in a lifetime, if that. Oh aye, that's the only way to describe it really. Everything, my whole life, everything, for those few minutes at least, it all fell into place, I'm telling you. Am I making any sense? I don't suppose I am but then again, these things aren't meant to make sense otherwise everyone would be at it and where would the fun be in that? The hammer was by the entrance in one of those sale baskets, everything inside was going for half price. We've one exactly the same at home so I knew what it was capable of all right. When I saw it there, sticking out amongst the dented tins and paint brushes I knew right there and then what I had to do. *Take me, take me* – well not exactly but you get the drift don't you? And I did take it, and I did what I had to do, and it was over in a couple of minutes and it felt great, really great, and I don't regret any of it, not one single iota, none of it. There's a saying for it, something about seizing the moment, seizing the day? Oh, and while we're at it, it was just the one bathroom unit, okay? Just the one unit, sink and bath with gold taps, toilet, medicine cupboard – there was even one of those bidet things you get in France; now you mention it, yes, very similar to the bathroom here come to think of it, apart from there being no bidet of course. Could've done with one of those things at school mind you, to clean your boots after football of course, what did you think? And as for all that nonsense about dead bodies all over the place, people do exaggerate, which is understandable I suppose when you think about it. When you put a two-pound hammer to a Royal Doulton there's bound to be a little dust, those things are built to last, you know . . . Oh for crying out loud, who's kidding who, eh? I mean, you've only one life, haven't you? I mean, you tell me, was it too much to ask for? To be great, like. That's all. That's all I ever wanted really. Not just your everyday greatness on the telly or the newspapers. Oh no. When I say great I mean Great. Great with a capital G. Great like scoring the winning goal in the European Cup Final, that kind of thing. There's only seconds left in injury time and Manchester United are level with Real Madrid and I've done the most amazing goal-saving tackle, literally clearing the ball off the line, after which I nonchalantly back-heel the ball to Georgie Best who then does an amazing run down the left flank, dummying one player after another, then he does an inch-perfect pass five yards to the other side of the pitch to Bobby Charlton who, without missing a blink, flicks the ball with his left instep right into the penalty box, and I'm there after having run from the other end of the pitch in eight seconds flat, which would have been a record if anyone had had a stopwatch handy, and just as the referee is about to blow the whistle I launch myself into the air to head the ball past the despairing hands of the goalkeeper. Then the referee blows the whistle and the crowd goes mad and the team does a lap of honour with Denis Law and Pat Crerand carrying me on their shoulders all the way, after which the team goes up to collect the European Cup from the Queen and I remember to wipe my hands on my shirt before shaking hands with Ma'am herself, as it would have been a right shame to have mucked up those lovely white gloves of hers. And in years to come the winning goal would be used on training tapes, history programmes and celebrity quiz-shows as the most perfect example of a header since sliced bread. Now that's what I call Great! Failing that, having the Christmas number one on *Top of the Pops* wouldn't have been bad, or what about winning the Nobel Prize in both Literature and Science after having discovered the direct link between rhyming couplets and the big-bang theory. Now that would have been nice.'

And there were no two ways about it really. You got a better standard of toilet in these four-star hotels in the middle of the Oxfordshire countryside. Sparkling fresh sinks and toilet bowls, clean enough to eat your dinner off. And if you weren't hungry then all you had to do was look at yourself in the mirror and tell yourself that joke again, the one about the US naval ship.

'The same joke I told to them Yanks the other day, Mutt and Jeff. I'm telling you, if looks could kill. Anyway, strictly speaking it's not a joke. It's an actual transcript of the radio conversation of a US naval ship with Canadian authorities off the coast of Newfoundland. Radio Four I think, *Pick of the Week*, or *Family Favourites*, I can't remember exactly. I'll tell it like I heard it, okay?

'*Canadians*: Please divert your course fifteen degrees to the South to avoid a collision.

'*Americans*: Recommend you divert your course fifteen degrees to the North to avoid a collision.

'*Canadians*: Negative. You will have to divert your course fifteen degrees to the South to avoid a collision.

'*Americans*: This is the captain of a US Navy ship. I say again, divert YOUR course.

'*Canadians*: No. I say again, you divert *YOUR* course.

'*Americans*: THIS IS THE AIRCRAFT CARRIER USS LINCOLN, THE SECOND LARGEST SHIP IN THE UNITED STATES' ATLANTIC FLEET. WE ARE ACCOMPANIED BY THREE DESTROYERS, THREE CRUISERS AND NUMEROUS SUPPORT VESSELS. I DEMAND THAT YOU CHANGE YOUR COURSE FIFTEEN DEGREES NORTH, I SAY AGAIN, THAT'S ONE FIVE DEGREES NORTH, OR COUNTER-MEASURES WILL BE UNDERTAKEN TO ENSURE THE SAFETY OF THIS SHIP.

'*Canadians*: This is a lighthouse – *your call!*'

Meanwhile, back at Samson Brothers, events in the car park had gathered at quite a pace. The Latin American classes were in full swing by now, so much so that the classes at Arthur Murray's school that evening had to be cancelled on account of the low attendance. And as for the card schools, well, the pot for the canasta game had risen to one thousand pounds, with the only players left being Rod Henry from the machine shop and Iris Temple, PA to Jack Deepes, Home Sales Director, who'd only been passing on her way to the vet with the dog to have his toenails clipped when she saw all the commotion going on and thought she'd pop over and have a look. And Kim Simms on the Ann Summers stall had never done such a roaring trade, with the double-headed vibrators going down like hot cakes, not to mention the fruit-flavoured g-strings, strawberry being the most popular with mango coming in a close second. And it was just as well the long queue for the hairdresser's booth had extended to Ali's newsagents on the Welston Old Road as the refreshment cart had run out of hot drinks and KitKats and the only reading material available was a 1973 Christmas *Bunty* annual and last year's annual accounts for the north-west branch of the Society of Orthodontists.

As far as Simon Standage was concerned, he'd only been following the rules and regulations as stipulated in the *Management Handbook*, and seeing as he was the most senior level of manager on site at the time, what the hell else was he supposed to do? But even Simon could see once the inquiries began that there had to be a scapegoat, the higher up the better, and it didn't take a lawyer to work out who it would be. It hadn't occurred to him that he'd been rubbing everyone's back up, and that unpopularity was part of his job – to be firm, to make a stand, not to back down. It was expected for a man of his position. Twenty-nine years old and Assistant Personnel Director, an office in the executive suite, six years out of law school, married six years with a little girl called Sadie, two years, a detached house in Marple Bridge. And to think that his mother had been so disappointed with him when he quit studying for a PhD in order to pursue a career in industry, or in the real world, as he said to her at the time.

'I said to her at the time, I said, *Listen Mother, I've been in education for all my life. School, university, postgraduate business school, it's all the same thing and to be frank with you,*

Mother, I've had it up to here. Regrets, are you kidding? I'd made my mind up and once you've made your mind up that's it. You take it on the chin, you don't look back, you be a man. You make your stand and you stick to it. No doubts whatsoever, not in the slightest, no sirree. Do you think I like being called a bastard? Do you think I like visiting someone in his hospital bed and telling him he hasn't got a job to come back to because of impending redundancies, in front of all his family? Oh no, I don't like being called a bastard but someone has to do it. Someone has to make the hard decisions, and if it has to be me then so be it. What's the point of pussyfooting about. That's what I don't understand about these lot. Just look at them. You make the decisions for them and what happens, they throw it right back in your face. I don't want to call them ungrateful but sometimes, I don't know, I wish I could wash me hands of them, I really do.'

It was Jane, his wife, who'd come up with the idea in the first place, and with those redundancies coming up, well. He and Jane weren't averse to starting something anew. And besides, they'd had their little plan for a long time now – that vegetarian café. And the redundancy money coming in, a full year's salary, not to mention the Government Enterprise grants available to start up new businesses, it all did seem possible. Jane could keep up her job as a college lecturer so there would be a regular salary coming in at least. And many years later, after awards for the best vegetarian café three years running, two more cafés, one in Deansgate and another in Marple Bridge, a six-figure offer from a nationally based burger franchise to buy the rights to the MegaVega burger specially developed by Simon himself, they decided that maybe now was as good a time as any to call it a day and retire to their five-bedroom villa in Magaluf.

But that was all to come and as far as Reg Prentice was concerned, this was a good time to cover your own back and pretty damn quick too because the shit was about to hit the fan. If there was one thing that twenty-two years experience had taught him, it was that at times like this it paid to have as many witnesses as was humanly possible, the more the merrier.

'. . . and let it be said that as far as I, Reginald Prentice, Senior Contracts Manager for eight years and second in command out here, the most senior being the Personnel Manager who is about to make an announcement, let it be said that I, Reginald Prentice, have no idea what the said Assistant Personnel Director is about to announce over the tannoy in a couple of minutes' time, and despite my repeated warnings, in spite of my appeals, and against my better judgement based on twenty-two years' experience, I might add, when he's worked out how the damn thing works . . . Oh hello Matt, didn't see you there.'

'Okay Reg, we heard you the first time,' said Matt. 'I've a cassette recorder in the car if you want it down on tape.'

'Is he stupid or what? At this rate he'll have a strike on his hands by four o'clock and it ain't even five past three,' said Lorna Smith.

Lorna Smith, married with two kids, had lately been finding herself looking at her reflection in the bathroom mirror longer than she ought to in the morning. Occasionally when she was feeling really masochistic she would take out a photo from the medicine cabinet which she kept close by for moments like this, when she felt like being just that extra little bit hard on herself. She'd take it out and there right in front of her was the same Lorna Smith, only nine years younger when she was eighteen and hadn't even met Frank yet. Almost the same hairstyle if truth be known, never a creature of fashion even at that age. If the photo could show the rest of her body then you'd see that her weight hadn't changed that much. A size eight without even trying, which was something at least. But that was nine years ago and now was a different matter altogether. The deep lines where there used to be a fresh face and sparkling eyes even before the makeup and foundation. And, if she isn't mistaken, a grey hair peeking out. The first of many, that was for sure.

'At times I think to myself, where did it go, where did it all go? Just like that. It just upped and went, didn't even say goodbye. Easy come, easy go, eh? Don't you believe a word of it, mate. When you look at your face in the mornings you sure as hell miss it. Where did that little girl go? I didn't think I was little at that age. I knew everything. We all do. But if only we knew, eh, if only we knew. Even so, that Simon Standage, the man's an idiot. Is he stupid or what?'

And in the end, the gun siege on Acomb Street ended as simply as it had begun. It was quite straightforward, actually, with all that infra-red ultrasound state-of-the-art weaponry with the precision to shoot the snot off a gnat's nose from a hundred yards downwind; once the gunmen had taken their places, it was pretty much all over bar the shooting – no pun intended – as Darren Molloy Pearson had refused point blank all requests to release the hostages immediately, put down the gun and come out with his hands raised, like they do on the telly.

Not that Sean McKay could give a tinker's cuss one way or the other. He'd only six months to go before retirement and the mortgage had been paid up for three years now. Still, looking at Simon Standage there, holding that megaphone and making a right idiot of himself, if his eyes wasn't deceiving him then things weren't all bad.

'Oh look, flares are back.'

nineteen

And in the distance, the St Martin's church bell struck a quarter to one as the last of Clive's funeral procession passed by. As funeral processions went, it was pretty bog-standard really, proceeding past the road alongside the factory and then to the main office gates. About a quarter of a mile in distance altogether, where the procession went after that was anybody's business. With twenty to thirty cars driving along at ten miles an hour, it was hard cheese for anyone wanting to drive out the car park in the lunch break. Still, it was Wednesday at least and no other processions were planned for the rest of the week, not to Personnel's knowledge anyway. And it was not a mistake they had any intention of repeating either, not after the last time, when everyone missed Don House's funeral procession in October in spite of the fact that his wife had phoned Personnel with the date and the exact time. A special edition of the in-house magazine had to be issued expressing the company's deepest and sincerest apologies to both family and friends, or else there would have been a lightning strike at the very least.

Not that it made any difference in the long run, and at least it gave the office staff something else to moan about for a couple of weeks or months if nothing else cropped up in between, which was highly unlikely, something else was bound to. And if not, then you made something up. It wasn't that hard, all it took was two people, and with a little time, imagination and bloody mindedness, you'd be surprised what you could come up with if you put your mind to it. And, as is the case with general chit-chat, you generally made up the rules as you went along. Any subject was fair game: the weather, neighbours, telly, sex, who'd died lately, sex; or preferably a combination of all of the above, which generally came under the heading of television. And if one of the participants happened to let slip something that they'd rather have kept secret which the other felt honour bound to tell all and sundry at the first available opportunity, then so much the better. Saying that, there had to be one rule at least, and that was an unwritten one, the one that went without saying. There'd been far too many casualties, Clive Barnes being the latest case in a long line since time immemorial. And unless you were absolutely stupid, or in Matt's case just having one of those *off* days which happens to everyone from time to time, then it was absolutely crucial to have good friends about you, like Henry and Irene, to help you get over those sticky moments, because you never knew when it might be your turn next.

'There are times,' said Matt, 'you know, when I have to

remind myself what I'm doing here in the first place. I mean, what am I? What do I do here? I know I've a job title but I mean, what does it mean, eh? Contracts and Procedures Draughtsman, I mean, what's that when it's at home? I get paid, I know that, me bank statement tells me every month, we've a caravan in Newquay and there's seven years left on the mortgage and the wife says I should cut down on butter, but apart from that, I mean, what else is there, tell me that, what else is there? And there's other times, more times than I care to mention actually, when all I want to do is scream and scream and scream till me head bursts.'

Moments like this were just begging for someone to jump in and take over the talking, and pretty damn quickly for Matt's sake before any permanent damage was done. Luckily Irene was on hand with just the right story to tell, having been to a wedding reception two weeks ago last Saturday.

'Everything was all right until the best man got up to do his speech. It started off okay with the usual stuff about drinking and ex-girlfriends; it was when he got to describing the stag night that matters went awry. Apparently the best man and the groom had been out clubbing one night when the groom suggested they go to this club in town, only the best man was surprised as he knows this is a well-known gay club but the groom insists, as it turns out the groom has a membership for this club and he's had it for two years now. Yes, the best man says this, in his speech, right in front of everyone. You could have heard a pin drop, I'm telling you, the look on the bride's face . . .

Talking of weddings, hey, isn't that Margery over there? Over here Margery. What's this I'm hearing about wedding bells then? I'll be getting an invite I hope.'

At the end of the day it's all about acceptance and loving yourself, Margery Watkins was fond of saying. If you couldn't love yourself then there was no hope, was there? Even so, marriage was a big step, nothing to sneeze at. A wedding was the most important day in a girl's life.

'Margery Elaine Watkins, HND with Distinction, Maltby College, Information Technology Officer, twenty-three years old, now look at me. When the right fellow comes along, I'm just like the rest.'

'Talking to ourselves now, are we?' said Matt. 'First sign of madness that, you know.'

'Sorry, Matt,' said Margery, 'I was miles away.'

'Well, you've a lot on your mind, haven't you?' said Henry. 'Have you set a date yet?'

'I haven't told him yet, give me a break, it's his first day.'

'Well, when you do decide on a date they do a great reception at the rugby club off Prince Street,' said Matt, 'Me mate's head barman there. The Palace Suite. I'll have a word and he'll get you a discount. Sit-down meal or finger buffet, I'll ring him tonight for a price list.'

'Tell me, Margery,' said Henry, 'I'm a bit behind the times. Is it the girl's father that does the paying or have they changed that as well?'

'Avoid balloons at all costs,' said Irene. 'It's a right bugger getting them off the dance floor. Oh, and another thing, have a look at the best man's speech before he reads it out.'

And after that the conversation between Margery, Matt and Henry followed its natural course, from weddings to houses to babies and families. Which was fine by Margery, as it gave her the chance to get things off her chest. Which was equally fine by Henry and Matt as both of them had always had a bit of a thing for Margery Watkins, if truth be known, and just watching and listening was more than fine by them. Which was just as well really as neither had any chance of getting a word in edgeways even if they'd wanted.

'All I've ever wanted was to marry and have six kids, that's all. Preferably six strapping sons, of course. All farmers, or cowboys or blacksmiths – like that film *Seven Brides for Seven Brothers*, yeah that one. And all I want to do is stay home and cook the meals for them and keep house of course. A little farm like *Little House on the Prairie*. And when they come from work all tired and sweaty, I'll make them wash of course, and change their clothes. And I'll have a good hearty meal on the table all ready for them. Roast chicken, peas, beans, coleslaw, and jugs of home-made lemonade. Yes, I can see it now. I'll make them say prayers of course, because we'll be a God-fearing family. The eldest will be James Junior. When they're older they'll go out *a'courting* with the local girls, each one of them; they'll be handsome boys, take after their father. And me and James, we'll sit by the fire just talking about old times and rocking in our chairs and stuff, doing a crossword puzzle, watching the telly, whatever takes our fancy, you get like that when you get to that age. What's that Matt? Does James get letters from the West Indies, with the stamps on? Since when have you collected stamps? I don't know, talk about still waters. Go on, ask him yourself, he's coming this way. Hey, James, over here, no here, yes darling, over here. You'll never guess what they've been saying about us, you'll only laugh . . .'

JOE PEMBERTON

Forever and Ever Amen

A magical depiction of a Moss Side childhood, with more musical numbers than *The Wizard of Oz*.

'James ia a vivacious young black boy, growing up in sixties Moss Side, whose daydreams feed into both British and Caribbean culture. He translates all aspects of his life into a fanfare, alive with music and dance [to tell] the tale of his family's emigration from St Kitts . . . brims with flavour' *The Times*

'Imagine *Billy Liar* rescripted on the premise of race instead of class, and you come close to the mixture of gritty realism and escapist fantasy that charges this debut with hypnotic energy . . . Excels at capturing the texture of its times. A *Catcher in the Rye* set in the semi-detached streets of Ashton-under-Lyne' Graham Caveney, *Sunday Express*

'This is a story that should be told and here is a fresh new voice to tell it' Hilary Mantel

0 7472 6241 1

review

MARK BARROWCLIFFE

Infidelity for First-Time Fathers

'Stunning – even better than his first' Jill Mansell

There's something wrong with Stewart Dagman's life. The party invitations used to read 'Bring bottles and First Aid kit. Eight till police raid.' Now they say 'Ben is one. Help us celebrate. Please leave quietly before afternoon nap.'

Life is moving on, and Dag wants to move with it. All he wants is someone to love, a family of his own and a half-indecent sex life.

So what happens when those dreams come true? Twice. In a week.

It's a tough life, being a modern man, dealing with girlfriends, parenthood, friendship, lollipop ladies, bloodhounds, parents, weddings and 6'8" gangsters called Dave the Lesbian. All whilst finding time for the annual lads' ski-ing holiday, of course . . .

'Mark Barrowcliffe is a master of recognition humour' Sue Margolis

And don't miss Mark Barrowcliffe's earlier bestseller, GIRLFRIEND 44

'I howled with laughter' *Mirror*

'A natural chronicler of the love-lorn male' *The Times*

'Hilarious . . . [Barrowcliffe is] an assured stylist with a lively, wordy wit' *Independent on Sunday*

0 7472 6815 0

review

SUSIE BOYT

The Last Hope of Girls

'Sometimes Martha wishes that her experience of family life was more like that of other people. Luckily for us, it's not, for the heroine of Boyt's third novel is a wonderful creation' *Marie Claire*

Newly installed as live-in caretaker of four Oxford Street flats, Martha Brazil can scarcely believe her luck. After years of stuffy bedsits and seedy suburban flatshares, the future seems electric with the promise of renovation and repair. Cruising her local department store by day, and thrilling to the sounds of revelry that float through her window at night, it strikes her that surely an independent young person with flair and a surplus of willpower ought to shine in such a setting.

But when out of the blue a copy of her father's latest novel falls into her hands, it offers Martha a view of her world, and of her wayward family, that she can only ignore at her peril.

Praise for *The Last Hope of Girls*:

'Unconventional, unsettling and beautifully written . . . Witty, laser-assisted vignettes suffuse *The Last Hope of Girls*' Lynne Truss, *Sunday Times*

'Boyt has a painter's eye for colour and detail . . . her text is as alive with symbolism as a Holbein painting . . . Very likeable' *Independent on Sunday*

'[A] touching, romantic tale of a young woman adrift amid the bright lights of London' *Mirror*

'A very sensitively observed novel, as though the central character has one less layer of skin than other people . . . Written with a very visual, almost painterly eye for detail' *Daily Mail*

'Thoughtful and emotional . . . A really meaty read' *Company*

0 7472 6515 1

review

PETER JINKS

Hallam Foe

Hallam has chosen an unusual teenage hobby: voyeurism. His interest is professional – less for sex than for intimacy, power, and to punish his father and stepmother for his mother's death. However, his mastery of treehouses and telescopes arouses suspicion, and he is banished to Edinburgh's medieval Old Town, where his voyeurism becomes more dangerous. However, Hallam is ceaselessly inventive, and skylights and rooftops have potential beyond his most romantic, and vengeful, dreams.

Outstandingly funny, gripping and strange, *Hallam Foe* is a masterpiece of idiosyncrasy and troubled youth.

'Superb . . . unusually exciting [and] amusing' *Scotland on Sunday*

'So terse and tense, so utterly packed with atmosphere, and potential to scare or excite, that you simply marvel at what Jinks can do' *Scotsman*

'A delight . . . Jinks should be applauded' *Sunday Herald*

0 7472 6748 0

review